Captain
Bennett's
Folly

Captain Bennett's Folly

by

Berry Fleming

℗

THE PERMANENT PRESS
Noyac Road, Sag Harbor, NY 11963

Library of Congress Number: 88-92466

International Standard Book Number: 0-932966-93-4

Manufactured in the United States of America

THE PERMANENT PRESS
Noyac Road
Sag Harbor, NY 11963

Captain Bennett's Folly

SOCRATES TO CEBES: *Still I suspect that you . . . are haunted with a fear that when the soul leaves the body the wind may really blow her away and scatter her; especially if a man should happen to die in stormy weather.*

1

Down in georgia in the summer-fall the hurricane girls go by as if competing in a talent show for Miss Tropical Disturbance—Delia, Ethel, Flora that year, and then Gilda; all of us at the box in our Kustom-Kitchen watching her 'slashing and clawing' at South Florida (after 'casting her roving eye all over the Caribbean, making passes at every land mass from the Leeward Islands to Cuba,' the anchor trying to modernize the Weather Bulletin with some lubricity).

Slashing and clawing, it seemed to us, straight for Uncle Nolan Bennett on Pelican Key. Stacy mumbled, No such luck, but nobody else heard him through the wind-whistles, whipping palms, horizontal rain, waterspout surf, and we went on being a little uneasy about Nolan, Nolan with one heart attack already and pushing eighty too—though he didn't seem to push very hard, 'eighty pulling Nolan' we called it, trying to make a joke of his longevity which with all the bequests hanging fire wasn't funny. Sisterbaby said, 'Call him!' and Mamma went to the phone and tried to but the

3

lines were down (next of kin she was, niece—'beloved niece,' the will would say—Iona Bennett when she married Papa, gone to his reward).

Then three or four days later, Gilda trying to start something with Cape Hatteras by that time, Stacy buzzed for me in the front office (Front Office), Stacy Vidrine my stepfather (VIDRINE & BIRLANT, REALTORS: 'Moving up? Settling down? See V-&-B.' *Beautiful Glenhaven Hills* was our baby). He didn't look up, just sat there with his hat on—one-inch brims that year, canary-bird feather in the band—wiggling the wet cigar at his pad. 'Message here when I got back from Kiwanis, call the operator at Oyster Key. This could be *it*, Walker, get on the other phone,' picking up the receiver and starting the wheels turning while I was saying, 'Nolan's on Pelican, Stacy,' (sometimes I called him 'Dad' but it killed him, young at heart).

He said the hospital might be on Oyster. 'Or, God forbid, the undertaker, just keep your shirt on—no, miss, I wasn't talking to you,' muttering 'you can take yours off' for my benefit, to remind me what a rascal he was, remind both of us. 'I imagine he'll want to be planted here with the family, you know how he is—was, I'm just thinking out loud now, it may not be the undertaker but who the hell else, except maybe the doctor, same thing,' rocking back with his chin in to run the upper lenses over our great plat of *Beautiful Glenhaven* on the wall and particularly I don't doubt over the engineer's neat letters spelling 'NOLAN BENNETT, ESQ., 27.6 ACRES' on the tract just west of us (The Home Place, Nolan called it) where Nolan had us blocked until the will could be processed, had the condo blocked, already named—*Chalet Regency*, one of Mamma's ironclad suggestions—plans drawn, money waiting to get to work (the bank's) interest rates climbing.

We needed the 27.6 now, not just any old time Nolan got round to an inter vivos or going under; we were pouring on our next to last lot, parcel, the house already sold, the U-HAUL up in Ohio ready to hook on. The City stopped us on the east, the River on the south, and the new six-lane on the north that was a feed-in for the Interstate a few miles out. Nolan's line was the only one with any flexibility, any 'give' as we put it (possibility of any). We had talked to him about it, the *give*, in a delicate backhanded way, Mammá had, the tax advantage of gifts to loved ones (his $30,000 Lifetime Exemption just sitting there as far as we knew), holding the estate down, screwing the Feds, not an easy thing to handle on a long-distance phone. He never got the point. Or seemed not to, hard to be sure with Nolan—looking both foreshort-ened and exaggerated to me beyond the Gap and making me feel that what I say about him now is almost hearsay though I knew every liverspot on his hands and cheeks; started talking, the last time, about 'a little shrimp boat down here for sale.' 'Little boat? Or little shrimp, Uncle No?' It didn't carry.

We had hardly seen Nolan in fifteen years, once since the heart attack and Dr. Arthur's 'Get away, Mr. Bennett' when Nolan was on his feet again, 'Complete change, get away from it all' (meaning us all as if we were viruses, not the good g.p.'s favorite family, and the other way round), Nolan submissively winding things up, cashing in a few acres of the Folly land down the river (I'll get back to that), cranking up and setting out, the pastures-new look growing in his eyes—eye, I should say, 'Where you going, Uncle Nolan?' we asked him, I did or maybe it was Sisterbaby. 'You got any place in mind, or you just going to let her roll?' He said, 'Schurz. I want to see Schurz.'

And off they went, Aunt Mat at the controls, enough to give anybody a seizure but he had some pills.

We had heard him speak of Schurz, met him once (twice, really), 'the finest noncommissioned officer in the United States Army'—Captain Bennett's First Sergeant, Battery B, 19th Field Artillery: 'Battery in camp at Spartanburg waiting for a commanding officer,' (Schurz filling us in, there on the front porch of The Home Place, watching it unfold in our faces). 'Captain walks in fresh out of Fort Knox (lieutenant then), forms the Battery. First thing he said was, "All right, you men, you can't run a war without a typewriter. Anybody here knows how to use a typewriter?" Hands go up but he sees me first. "What's your name, Soldier?" "Private Schurz, sir." "Where you from?" "Milwaukee, sir." "Wife and children?" "No sir." "Typewriter's in the office, Schurz." '

'Remember all those potatoes, Schurz? Ten years after the Armistice I still couldn't eat potatoes.'

'Three days out of Norfolk on a converted freight boat carrying potatoes, my God, *influenza!* "Stay out in the air, Lieutenant." Fixed him a corner in the bags where he could sleep, potatoes kept the wind off. Convoy on the southern route to dodge the U-boats, hotter every day, bodies stacked four deep on deck, what do you do? Lieutenant reads the burial service, over they go. Dock at Saint-Nazaire, hike on to camp at Angoulême. . . . Battery on a ridge, pulling out, sun going down . . .' And so on, until our fidgetings and squirmings shook the old 2 x 12s under the floor.—He sent Nolan a birthday card from Wisconsin every June for thirty-one years: *'Birthday Cheers, Captain!' 'Ninety-nine Happy Returns of the Day!' 'Health and Long Life to the Captain!'* the usual thing—square as a concrete block.

When there was no card on the thirty-second Nolan started waiting every day at the mailbox to make Mr. Thompson try a little harder. 'Not today, Mr. Nolan,' clutch out for a light-and-rest-your-saddle. 'Dear me, Thompson, I hope nothing's happened to Schurz, the finest noncommissioned officer . . .' and into it again.

He was on the blue-and-white-speckled front steps one morning coming back from the box when a car and trailer pulled up in the sandy yard with a load of towheaded passengers and a basket of pigeons tied on top of the trailer: 'Who's this! My God, it's Schurz!'

'CAPTAIN!'

He had sold out his business and was headed for Florida where he and the pigeons could get warm, a solid bald little man five or six years younger than Nolan and as many inches shorter and pounds heavier. After that the cards began coming from the Keys—from, I wasn't quite sure but almost was, Oyster Key.

I tried to break it to Stacy but I was too late. 'Who?' said Stacy. 'What's the name? Shoes? Shows?' then, 'Oh!'

Schurz said he was calling 'about the Captain' and Stacy revived enough to say, 'Nothing serious, I hope.' Schurz said, 'Well, sir—' and Stacy cut in with, 'Not another attack!' in his don't-tell-me voice, giving me a hold-everything-now flat of the hand as if sure I would bumble in and scare the thing off the hook.

Schurz said, Well, no sir, not exactly and Stacy asked him what he meant by not exactly. 'I mean I've never seen the Captain quite like this before.'

'Like what, Mr. Schurz? What does he do?'

'Oh, nothing special, it's not that so much, what he does—'

'As what he doesn't do? Yes? What doesn't he do?'

'I couldn't really—'

'What seems to be—the doctor, what does the doctor say?'

'No sir, it's not that kind of thing.'

'What kind of thing IS it, Mr. Schurz?'

Schurz said it was hard to say, he just thought the family ought to know and Stacy swallowed his 'Know WHAT, for

Christ sake?' to ask if Nolan was in the hospital. 'No sir, he's
at home. Says he feels good. But he doesn't get much sleep,
that is, he sleeps but it doesn't rest him. He's been having
bad dreams.'

'Everybody has bad dreams nowadays, Sergeant. I'm
scared to go to bed at night.'

'Trouble is the Captain doesn't think they're dreams.'

Stacy said, 'Oh, well, now!' throwing me a look as if I
wouldn't have caught the significance of that. 'Well, er,
that's not too good now, Mr. Schurz, is it? you ought to
be able to tell the difference,' giving the cigar a couple of
thought-raps on the solid-gold ash tray Mamma had brought
him from Australia one Christmas (the only thing she could
think of he didn't have). Schurz started to say something
but Stacy broke in to ask if there was a shrink on the Keys.

Schurz didn't understand. 'From the blow? No sir, there
wasn't much damage.'

'If there isn't I suppose I could have Dr. Mollenbrink
come down there check him out, bastard's high as a kite
though'—a new-arrival in town with the industries, five or
six years, has one of our splits on Zinnia Circle, not a sure-
enough shrink, a psychologist, MARRIAGE COUNSELOR
his card reads (three times divorced, so he knows the problem—problems—three alimonies nothing in his life with
book royalties flushing him out of house and office from his
Current Sex Techniques, in which 'never before revealed
facts transform the staleness, apathy and boredom of the
sexual act into the thrilling, fulfilling, ecstatic moments you've
always read about,' Sisterbaby has it in paperback from
college).

'No sir, he feels good, looks good.'

'Well, in that case, Sergeant——'

'Mrs. Littleberry takes care of everything.'

'I see. Well, in that case, Mr. Schurz, what's on your—aren't we just throwing away your good nickel?'

'I just thought the family——'

'Is this some neighbor of his I take it, Mrs. Littleberry?'

Schurz said Mrs. Littleberry was the Captain's housekeeper and Stacy said, I see, again, then juggling Mrs. Littleberry back and forth not knowing quite where to lay her down, 'Where's *Mr.* Littleberry, Sergeant?' Schurz said it was *Lieutenant* Littleberry (the place sounded like a Veterans Hospital) and he had died on the way home from Germany.

'Well, well, is that so?'

'Buried at Key West.'

'I see. And the Lieutenant's widow is making herself useful round the house?'

'Yes sir, neat as a pin. German, Swiss, Scandinavian maybe. Trims his hair.'

Stacy said excuse him for laughing but he thought Schurz said she trimmed his hair and Schurz said, 'Found some small-animal clippers on a shelf in the dock house when we were painting the boat and oiled them up and——'

'You have a boat?'

'The Captain, yes sir. You see——'

'How old is she, Mr. Schurz?'

'The boat? I don't really——'

Stacy said, 'Look, Mr. Schurz, here's what I'm going to do. Strange enough it just so happens that Walker—you remember Walker Williams, in business with me now' (I was a salesman, *the* salesman)—'Walker has a business appointment in Miami next week' (news to me) 'and I'm going to let him run down there on the Keys and see you all for a day or two. We love Nolan, you know, miss him, think about him all the time, tell him when you see him, tell him we tried to get him the other night but the lines were down. Worried about him—him and Gilda' (giving it a squirt of sex in case somebody might think he wasn't educated).

Schurz said Nolan didn't know he was calling, he hadn't told him, didn't want to upset him; which somehow seemed to make Stacy think it might not be Schurz's nickel after all but his and he began backing away from the phone to help break the connection, tossing in a few severing waves-of-the-hand phrases and in a minute laying it down.

It was an exaggeration, that thinking about Nolan all the time, but the lot we were pouring on was next to The Home Place and we did think about him every time we looked up from the footings and saw his barbwire fence, or looked across it at the old jigsaw house crying for a bulldozer (round-cornered porch with a candle-snuffer roof, that sort of thing) and the 27.6 acres of underdeveloped counter-culture woods and wildness and dead-beat rabbits and self-centered quail that were a torment to Stacy, and to the rest of us too in varying degrees, like the one oil companies feel looking at an undrilled ocean. He was like the man I've read of somewhere bound and gagged in a roomful of strippers. I've seen him glance over there and have to hide his eyes.

Because things had been happening in our town since Nolan's day. New industries, new people, new liquor stores, new houses, new garbage trucks, shopping centers, drive-ins, smashups, superhighways through what looked like Hamburger Heaven, overpasses, underpasses, bypasses, cotton fields modernized into subdivisions; you could almost see the half-starved lines of boll weevil refugees pushing farther west. *Beautiful Glenhaven* had been laid out on corn land Mamma had from Grandpa Bennett, Nolan's brother (a considerable hope chest from Stacy's point of view though he may have had other reasons for marrying Mamma too); Gopher Hill was the old name, which naturally wouldn't do. It was a bigger parcel than The Home Place, which went to Nolan, but Grandpa had balanced it out for Nolan by leaving him the tract down the river called Bennett's Folly, two thousand acres and a liability at the time what with taxes and being under water three or four times a year from the river-floods and nothing on it but swamp trees and wandering cows and a few small undernourished alligators, nobody having any notion old Senator Jim would get such a half-nelson on the Administration one day they would send down the Corps of Engineers and throw in a dam upstream that prevented the floods and turned the water blue and certainly no notion that Northern Industry would start piling in that liked having a river by the door to dump everything in. Stacy had closed a deal on a few acres of it for Nolan when Dr. Arthur told him to get away, the only land Nolan had ever parted with and he wouldn't have parted with that but for the emergency and probably being a little shaky too; money meant nothing to Nolan compared with land (I remember the way he folded up the don't-fold-staple-spindle-crease Yankee check). He wouldn't have sold us The Home Place if we had been fools enough to get so exasperated as to try to buy it. 'Land's thicker than money,' he used to say, 'and getting thicker all the time.'

As I say, we did get exasperated enough to bring out the give-now-save-later angle which he couldn't seem to get the straight of. At first we thought he wanted to keep it to give Aunt Mat a place she could return to when he had gone to his glory if she didn't like the Keys (which she had given every indication she didn't intend to, Schurz included) but when he brought her home for burial three or four years later we saw something of him (he and Schurz stayed at a motel not wanting to open The Home Place for so short a time—he wouldn't stay with us, said he was too old to be

12

anybody's house guest but I think he really found us tiresome in a kindly long-suffering way) and though we gave out all sorts of hints about needing the 27.6 he went back to the Keys without ever grasping the idea—went by train (trains then), ten times longer but he said he could think better on a train.

I remember I said, 'What you gonna think about, Uncle Nolan?' Mamma kicking at me under the table as if I was smudging a plus clause in the will.

Nobody could say he didn't answer the question—cocked his head to one side, squinted off for a minute not at but in the direction of Mamma's Hong Kong gong (not offended by the sass or more likely not recognizing it) then began by saying he was thinking his way into a mathematical system roughly comparable to differential calculus. 'I hope to contrive, Walker,' he said, 'a method for measuring the relationship between reason and unreason.'

I suppressed my gulp and said, 'Yes sir,'—what else can you say to a testator? (History had been his field at the University before he lost the sight of one eye but mathematics had always interested him; walked into a broken twig on a dogwood tree one night going home to Aunt Mat from a course he was taking in Arabic on the side because he had seen a picture of the dome of the mosque of the Shah of Isfahan and admired the caligraphy).

'To first analyze and systematize the vast areas of feeling—instinct, impulse, insight, dreams, intuition—and then by a sort of infrared symbolic logic to relate the areas to reason. I call it Incalculus, Walker, as a working title; it's fundamentally a study of the utterly incalculable.'

And I said, Yes sir.

'Present-day education, such as it is, is of, for, and by the mind, but that's just scratching the surface. These other things fly circles round the mind, do it every day. Not to say every night. Which is where my other project ties on.'

'Another project!' says Stacy, and Nolan says he doesn't like to bore us and Stacy comes back with, 'Not at all, sir; fascinating!' in the low-pitched buttering-up-a-client tone.

'Your eye movements when you dream, Stacy, tally with the dream's content; dreaming of going up stairs your eye movements lift up step by step.'

'I see,' says Stacy, falling over himself.

And being picked up by Nolan's 'Just a minute now. My project is to take the tracings of these eye movements, REM we call them, and transpose them, first, into sound waves, which they very much resemble, enabling one to *hear* one's dreams. Just a minute now. By then converting the sound waves into shades of gray I expect to obtain a visual image of the dream showing a broad spectrum of emotions from black to white. With some further refinements, expanding the emotional grays into the actual dream incidents that caused them, I hope to get a specific reproduction on motion-picture film of the dream itself, the entire dream, Stacy, not just the fast-fading wisps one now tries to hold on to. Imagine being able to project one's unconscious on to a movie screen!'

Stacy said, Staggering—meaning, in his case, terrifying.

'Breaking through the awareness barrier into inner space!' hands up stiff with a wacky excitement, then going on, 'Why bother with dreams? you say,' (nobody had opened his mouth—except to get more air). 'But one must dream, or his physical and psychic wellbeing will suffer. Sleep alone merely answers the needs of everyday biological living but dreams nourish ideas, imagination, spirit; sleep for the body, dreams for the spirit. And hear this, my dears! As sleep provides a garden for dreams to grow in, the body's purpose is to provide a garden for the spirit . . . .'

Naturally we thought of Nolan as, well, balmy is perhaps too strong (I'm not sure, or wasn't) and eccentric is not right, extraterrestrial maybe. With one foot in the grave it was as if he had also packed one lobe of his brain in his suitcase, his 'valise,' his 'Gladstone,' his 'carpetbag,' not shut it away completely perhaps but tucked it in there ready to move at the drop of a hat. For me even then there was something spooklike about Nolan in that, with his age and apparent friability, the thinness and luminosity of his skin, you felt you could almost see into him and at the same time hardly see him at all. Mollenbrink would have flipped out plenty of screw-starved sexplanations if he had ever met Nolan, been with him for a minute and a half, a fast explainer. Or met Aunt Mat. And certainly it would be asking a lot of the imagination to try to picture Nolan at a moment of being what Mollenbrink likes to call sexually gratified ('ful-filled,' sometimes, the fill-her-up-with-regular school). And if gratification is the payoff Nolan should have been in analysis or at least under sedation for, with all his bloom, he had without doubt been shortchanged. Yet you have to admit you see people with cartwheels of gratification round their eyes slamming into the analyst's parking lot as if they have diarrhea or hemophilia; I don't know the answer. Nolan might have benefitted from some recharging on the couch, some tightening of nuts and bolts, but he didn't seem to feel any need of it.

'. . . and if the train is late I want to go over what I've been thinking about evolution and the human spirit, *of* the human spirit.'

'I sure hope she's on time, Uncle No,' I said, throwing in the jollity that we in the Confederacy like to disrupt things with when they're clearly getting out of hand but that in this case Stacy received with a baleful stare at me bordering on malignant and 'Fascinating, Mr. Bennett!'

'Perhaps evolution, Stacy, is not linear but cycloidal, not a line, as we assume, but an arrangement of evolving circles—'

'Very interesting, sir.'

'—a sea creature crawling out of the surf, climbing the rocks, the cliff, ledge-to-ledge, up and up for a trillion years until he reaches the plateau and stands erect on the crest as Christ or Gautama or Shakespeare, then on to the downslope and over the secret edge into the sea again,' and other shit like 'inching gaily toward the brink today, a tattered coat upon a stick with no soul left to sing and louder sing . . . .' Anyhow, it was clear enough Nolan wasn't going to get on the train and start thinking about parting with any more land.

The *Beautiful Glenhaven* one-vacancy land was close in and hilly, not affected by Senator Jim's dam, except the dam meant industry and industry meant people (vice-presidents, managers, supervisors, engineers, technicians, scientists, sales-advertising-and-marketing men, PR experts, lobbyists, lawyers, coordinators, marriage councilors) who wanted houses; one of my most everyday expressions was, or had been, 'Watch the wet paint, Madam,' the places gone before we had a chance to wash the windows—Oxford Court, Cambridge Circle, Harvard Avenue, Princeton Road, and when we ran short of colleges we switched over to flowers and trees, each house different from the one next to it but the cluster itself repeated, reversed and shifted about in various ways like Beethoven and Bach, the four different houses in Rosebud Lane popped up mirrored in Pineneedle Road, good water-shedding immobile homes in their way (we aimed at having them peak at about four years, under the second owner, slipping a little after that until Glenhaven Builders, wholly-owned subsidiary, could get there with solder and jacks and roofing cement and caulking compounds and the usual finger-in-the-dike stuff). The next-to-last lot we were pouring on then was in Oleander Drive. I happened to be

in the office when Stacy phoned for the mixer: 'Oleander
Drive, end of the road,' he told the order clerk and sat
there with his hand on the instrument for a minute mumbling,
'End of the road,' as glum as if he had just bought a ceme-
tery lot.

Not that we were really against the wall. Stacy carried
some notes at the bank as a matter of policy, keeping his
credit flexible, ran a mortgage on the house of course (we
lived in Sorbonne Circle, in the older section), but he could
have bailed out, given a little time and a dash of luck; we
operated on the principle it was good business to wade in
as deep as the bank would let you, which Nolan was too
dated to comprehend even when Stacy diagrammed it, as he
did once when we thought Nolan might be talked into
borrowing fifty Gs on Bennett's Folly and joining the firm
(a backhanded way of sewing up The Home Place, among
other things), Nolan a pay-as-you-go man, skittish about
debt the way girls used to be about bedding down. We
weren't what you would call In Want. Our driveway looked
like a death in the family if we all happened to be home at
once—Mamma's Coupe de Ville, Stacy's Tempest (wide
track), the cook's Gran Torino, my own Mustang, Sisterbaby's MG, the yardman's Edsel. We had all the fridges,
freezers, color TVs, blenders, juicers, toasters, can openers,
electric carving knives and pencil sharpeners and hedge
clippers and auxiliary bathroom heaters, electric guitars and
clocks, a portable electric saw—all on time of course, which
gave the money people something to do, a chance to be
friends (as their sign reads, 'Helping is what friends are
for') but even more important kept the market bubbling,
kept the GNP tilted forward the way you tilt when you
walk or run, ('Or fall,' was Nolan's medieval response, unable to get to first base with grasping the promises-economy,
hung up on the mildewed notion promises are meant to be

kept so how are you any better off? not understanding you don't 'keep' promises, you promise again, pay off one promise with a new one, refund it like a municipal bond—you couldn't get anywhere trying to show him how wearing out the thing before you bought it kept you always a step ahead, telling us once something like we reminded him of Panurge eating his corn whilst it was still but grass, which was supposed to knock our teeth out). We had everything that could live on 110 volts and a lot that couldn't, washing machines, dish washers, dryers, air conditioners; sometimes a thunderstorm would short out a transformer and we would sit there in the sudden dark stillness as if kicked unconscious, but it wouldn't last long. There was enough affluence around to aggravate my itch for a blue-and-white Twin Comanche B tagged at sixty-two five hundred, affluence enough to let us be good-natured about Sisterbaby's spitting on the new Buick Special Mamma bought her so she could go to college to be with her friends, make new ones (in the back seat), (she preferred a fourthhand MG that had passed down from class to class like the faculty and was holding up better—except maybe the Driver Education Professor that she had a thing on at the time and gave a set of hub caps to), and enough to send Mamma off when the travel ads of the airlines and steamship lines had worked her into a frenzy like cattle prods (on and on, cruise after cruise, flight after flight, Great Circle, Little Circle, coming home as footsore and irritable as the Wandering Jew—Stacy may have had some place to put it but I doubt it, sex mostly talk with him, and only that because it was the IN topic). I mean we didn't need Nolan's money in a worldly way, or the barrels of it we could have turned The Home Place into, we needed it in a less material sense, for itself alone, BECAUSE IT WAS MONEY. Because it was 'there.' It gets on your nerves to have something like that stretched out behind a fence doing nothing. Thumbing its nose at you.

'How soon can you go?' Stacy said, studying the Cartier desk-clock as if he had right this minute in mind, it was a little after three.

I told him he had mentioned 'next week,' I thought I could manage next week, but when this almost exploded him I changed it to 'Tomorrow? Tomorrow morning?' I didn't want to go at all, Sisterbaby just getting in the clear again, but I could see the stakes. 'I promised Sisterbaby I'd take her to the picture show tonight' (picture show!). 'Tomorrow's only Wednesday.'

He said, 'You don't have to tell me the day of the week, Walker,' still jumpy, and I said, What did I do when I got there? trying to steer him into thinking ahead.

'Do? You take a good look around at everything and everybody—*including Mr. Schurz*—and phone me the score, sneak off down to the corner drug and phone in. That's simple enough, isn't it? Touch all the bases' (he was full of those moth-eaten once on-the-ballisms that were like the loud tweed jacket he had had at business school and still wore because he couldn't realize where the time could have gone). 'After that you play it by ear.'

I cringed at the p-by-e coming on top of the t-all-the-b but said okay.

'Run a memo on everything. If he's buggy, really buggy—at last—and starts monkeying with the will we'll want some hard facts to show when we take it to court.' I asked him where *was* the will anyhow? and he opened a drawer as if it were inside and pulled out a couple of the small *Beautiful Glenhaven* plats and a xerox of the architect's rendering of *Chalet Regency*. 'Take these along. Put your SOLD stamp on the stuff that's gone (everything!). Don't press him, you just thought he might be interested in our crucifixion—I

don't know where the will is, find out while you're there—
let him see for himself the fix we're in. Don't push him or
he'll go the other way. Easy does it. The soft sell.'

I asked him what I was selling and he said, 'Are you
here, Walker! You're selling tax-advantage. You're selling
brackets. You're leading him up to catch on all by himself
that giving your mother The Home Place now—and maybe
a hunk of the Folly land, or all of it for God's sake, why
not? she'll get it anyhow—is a hell of a lot cheaper than
making her inherit it, buy it back from the IRS. You're
selling Gift Tax against Estate Tax.'

I pointed out Nolan wouldn't give a damn about the estate
tax, wouldn't be here to take part in it, and he said, 'Keeping
it away from the Feds, saving his kin people, his loved ones.
You're selling kinship, benevolence, family ties, blood's-
thicker-than-water. And you're selling doing-it-now. If Continental Can gets the tax-shelters they want they're coming
in here and we're——'

It seemed to remind him of bad dreams because he jumped
over to Nolan's. 'What's giving him bad dreams, Walker?
no wife, no business, no children, not a worry in the world.'
A rhetorical question but I went along, showed empty hands,
said, Humidity? Diet? High tides? Gilda? Equinox? did it
matter? He said, 'You left out one,' giving me the raised
eyebrow that pronged up anyway from sleeping on that side.
'You left out housekeeper.'

I couldn't help laughing. 'Oh Stacy!' He *would* come up
with something like that, Tuesday Kiwanis more fun to him
than some people get out of a massage parlor but covering
it up with any wornout bawdiness he could think of.

'I've heard of old fools marrying housekeepers for less
than a haircut. How old *is* Nolan?'

I said I didn't know but he went way back. I remember
years ago Nolan looking at a picture in the *Times* of Senator

Jim being honored for something or other and reminiscing, 'Old Jim! I knew him when he was just a crook.' I told Stacy foot-in-the-grave was all I knew (all that mattered) and he said that wasn't too old to get notions. 'And if that's why the ball bounces, Walker, I'll come down there myself. Maybe bring your mother to reason with him. Maybe bring Livonia' (he can't stand calling her 'Sisterbaby'), 'he's always liked Livonia—I'm just thinking aloud now—she'd be a lot cheaper than Mollenbrink.'

I said it might be an idea to send 'Livonia' along with me now, let her get started, voice in a croak at the thought of it, us two vibrating through the blue with a pocket now and then like a 40,000-foot orgasm—a chubby round-faced girl with a curious delayed-fuse sort of sex (I almost said booby-trapped) that hit you all the harder because you had probably been concluding this was only a little fat girl. We had been overwhelmed by so much proximity soon after she came back home, by the simple convenience of everything, the underfootness, one roof, thin walls you could almost see through, I could hear her turn over in bed, (she had gone with Papa—Oedipus and all that—when Mamma kicked him out and we hadn't seen her for nearly twelve years; had been living with her stepmother, Papa long gone, but when the stepmother began work on a new prospect, a retired warrant officer with a pension, she was obviously in the way, the s.m. not taking to having an eighteen-year-old running round the house giving the man what Stacy called notions—incidentally, I'll never forget Papa when Mamma said, 'Why in hell don't you quit the stuff? You couldn't possibly like the taste,' and Papa said, 'Honey, I'd pour it over my grits every morning for breakfast if it wasn't so damn expensive'; neither here nor there). She was no part of the brat that had left us, not really fat, solid—knees that seemed to carry about the same pressure as my front tires—on the silent

side, walking in the door in wire-rimmed granny glasses
(for disguise hitchhiking) that she took off after we made
her welcome and forgot about; I was about thirty at the
time. I know there are still some old hats who are stiff-
necked about this sort of thing, particularly when it's within
the family, as if it hadn't been going on since the year one;
I even suggested to her impulsively once that we just pull
up and go to another town and get married—with a little
shenanigans here and there I believe we could have done it.
She refused, quite a self-willed person; 'If all these colored
people are going to be free I'm certainly not going to chain
myself to a grocery cart like a dog' (this was way before
women mobilized), taking a load off my mind, I had made
the offer. We got along well, she had the paperback—
autographed now with a somehow nervy 'Yum-yum, Mollenbrink.' (Before I forget it, there was nothing 'going on'
between her and Stacy; he was in the same position as the
warrant officer the stepmother had worried about but he
could take it, was more interested in a full bankbox than a
full bra—not Sisterbaby's fault, who can no more keep her
eyes off a man's zipper than a birddog can take his off a
nest of quail.)

He put his foot down on sending Sisterbaby but for straight-
out money reasons, said he didn't go for killing one bird
with two stones, could I handle it or not? and I said of
course I could handle it.

'Attaboy. You better go today. Call the field see how
soon you can get out.' He saw I didn't like the 'today' much
and said, 'On the company, Walker, expense account, you're
going down there to get hold of a piece of real estate, aren't
you?' as if arguing with himself (or Birlant). And then,
'Suppose we say there might be twenty-five bucks in it for
you if you bring home the flag.'—Twenty-five degenrate
bucks!

I said, 'Might be?' not to bicker over the insult in the light of 'expense account,' and, pushed, he said, 'Is' (meaning are).

I tried to tighten it one more notch by saying I'd have to rent a car at Miami of course, but he said, 'Bus goes right through Pelican, no way to miss it without drowning everybody,' switching then, to take my mind off the car, 'What about this Schurz character, Walker? Is he trying to get a foot in the door too? Get in a codicil? A new will, for God's sake!'

I told him Schurz had cashed in a lumber business, didn't need our money (Nolan's, to split hairs); 'Schurz has plenty of money.' He said if so that would be *one* man that had, unless I had plenty, which would make *two*, letting his bare third finger flick across the coal of his cigar two or three times which usually meant that ought to take care of you but if you want more there's more where that came from. I said if Schurz was up to anything why would he call the family? Which seemed to hold water and gave us both some relief, about as much as an aspirin. He said, 'There's the phone, call the field.'

2

IT WOULD HAVE BEEN a lot better for all of us in the long run if he hadn't been so tight about the car, I mean I would have given a better first impression, half the fight, because I would have driven straight on to Pelican when the plane set down and wouldn't have, as Nolan would say, 'got in with the wrong crowd' in Miami. As it was, the last bus had gone, next one 10:36 in the morning, and I had to spend the night as best I could—nothing out of the way, some rather plush tables the taxi driver was peddling where I fell in with a widow and her beachboyfriend and ended up at a drink place with topless people leaning them over the table to clear it and taking your order with one of them breathing in your ear, the beachboy reacting to them for some Freudian reason by taking a psychopathic swipe at me across the table; not anything much, scuffed cheekbone, hardly any blood, a couple of band-aids from the widow's evening bag took care of it, but it annoyed her and when he went to the men's room we left him with the bill and went on to another place and didn't get to bed until almost daylight, I mean no hard stuff or orgies or police trouble just everyday alcohol and innocent fun. But I forgot to leave a call and didn't wake up until the widow started on it again about five minutes to ten.

I stumbled on to the bus with the driver trying to close the doors in my face, no breakfast, no shave, and worst of all no chance to brush my teeth; no chance to notice my eye socket was getting blue until I glanced at his rearview by the door as I asked him if he stopped at Pelican and he snapped, 'Twelve-forty-one,' as if it were a quiz and I might be an inspector in a knocked-up disguise. It was then 10:37 (if we had to split seconds), two hours and four minutes of split-second blessed sleep, the man dieseling out from under the shed into a back street of cutout Miami shadows and then saying, 'Largo, folks, time for a smoke,' and it was 11:49 as if we had crossed a time zone, my eyes opening and closing again with a sort of rubber seal like the doors, and the sequence cutting to 'Pelican, you there, shake him, will you, Mister?' and a voice like mine saying, 'For God's sake don't shake me,' the purple plastic water circling everything, and the sun and sand and bridges and loafing sea birds, and a pain in your eyeballs as if the lid had been snatched off the box.

I got off with a sense of being unwanted but otherwise all right except for the glare like a tourniquet round your head, Pelican not much bigger than a garbage scow, hardly more than a touching-down spot for the straightaway bridges or a long-distance heron, the bus already gone and me there with half-a-dozen houses that the blacktop shot between at about roof level and the diamond-studded water everywhere.

I asked the sun-dried woman at the gift shop (Mrs. Maple, though I didn't know it then) which house was Mr. Bennett's and she said, 'Bennett? Bennett?' as if I had hit the wrong Key, then, 'Oh, the Captain!' and came to the door and pointed at 'Right yonder where you see the prowler,' scaring out of me something like 'Christ! The fuzz?' which I changed to 'the law' when she gave me the suspicious-character look. I said, 'Is he in some kind of trouble, Mr. Bennett?' thinking rather that if Nolan had had a sudden attack and the ambulance had screamed in it was possible the fuzz might have nosed in too, the flasher still and dull on the roof like a chained-up watchdog but scaring you to death just the same.

She said 'Ashalom' often stopped in if business was bad. 'They like to gabble about the Highway, he's leaving,' Ashalom appearing gray-hat-first up the slope from the yard then gray shirt then black belt, part of the roof behind him and the tops of some palm trees pushed out of kilter by the winds.

I didn't want to see him any closer (double band-aid curling at the edges on so much Keys-sweat, denim eye and all that) and I asked her if she had a checkroom inside I could check my suitcase—it was heavier every time I lifted it. She said, 'Set it in there, nobody bother it,' looking hard at the eye as if she might whistle for Ashalom; but she let him go and when I came back the car was pea-size on the southwest bridge and shrinking fast. I said, 'You want to give me a sort of check or something, you know?' and she said, 'Nobody bother it, what's a matter with you?' and I apologized—not much in it to bother.

Nolan was at a table in a rustling piece of shade from the trees leaning over him like those old-time gooseneck reading lamps. I might not have known him but for N. BENNETT on a mailbox, eleven years balder, beard now white of course. From a distance he didn't look very sick, forehead a kind of salt-cured blackened yellow like the trunk of a palm, clean white shirt, white duck seagoing pants, work shoes that looked like J. C. Penney. He scooped a calico cat out of his lap when he saw me and stood up but before I could say anything he turned off with a wave to follow him, the cat halfway up the far side of a tree by then as if allergic to me.

'First thing is to get back on course,' over a white shoulder; 'all this trash from last week I want you to rake it up in a pile and burn it, what you can't burn dig a nice hole over there back of the boathouse and bury it, shovel in the tool shed, rake, broom, wheelbarrow, everything you need' (I had been thinking Schurz was an alarmist but I began to beg his pardon), 'if you want something you don't see just holler——'

I said, 'I don't believe you know me, Uncle Nolan,' and he said, 'Have you worked for me before?' (the 'Uncle Nolan' didn't lead him anywhere), and I said who I was, said I'd been in Miami on a real-estate deal and thought I'd grab a bus and stop in for a minute to see how he was getting on.

'Walker? Goodness me! Schurz promised to send me somebody to clean up a bit, I let Chak off for a few days to go up to the powwow, we had a little blow last week. Come over and sit down, you don't look—are you all right, Walker? in good health? You look a little—but of course everybody else looks foot-in-the-grave to someone living on the Keys.'

Foot in the grave! Whose foot—I mumbled something about a pocket over Jax threw me against the corner of a seat but he said he was thinking more of the color of my skin, said his sainted mother used to give the children calomel for that sort of thing when he was a boy, nasty stuff, sending the old days a fond shake of the head that I cut short to save us from a pocket into the prehistoric. I asked him how he had been, tossing it off but watching his hands for telltale shakes or twitches or trembles I could report back to Stacy waiting to grab them, and not seeing any. 'You're looking fine,' I said as heartily as I could, back to thinking Schurz had been overanxious. He was thin but then he had always been thin; he didn't look the six-foot-one he used to claim, the years having worn him down a little, worn a little of the tread off, but no amount of watching for the silver lining could have suggested he looked sick. In fact he reminded me of an entry in an antique-car parade, obviously a long-dis- continued model but polished to a shine and chugging in a subdued easy rhythm that might go on indefinitely, using hardly a drop of gas, not many valves but all of them tapping.

For him, sitting down in his chair seemed to be returning to a nest of thoughts and he said, 'Ashalom and I—he patrols the bridges, knows every crack in the concrete, fine boy— we were just talking about that wonderful road out there, Walker.' I remembered spots in it that had bounced my cringing head but I said I agreed with him (I certainly hadn't come down there to be disagreeable). 'The particularity of it, Walker, the no-forks, the no-crossroads to confuse you, the naught-besidedness,' Yes sir. 'You go that way, or you go *that* way. You go Sunup, or you go Sundown. Forward or back, right or wrong, day or night, life or death, true or false.'

I said, 'Gin or whisky,' and he smiled, tolerating limitations in the guest—if he had really heard me.

'You don't go off on a side road hoping you can have it both ways, you make your choice, one way or the other, up or down, up's harder than down as you might expect."

I couldn't imagine the fuzz sitting there letting such crap pile up round his chin; 'What does the fuzz say?'

'Fuzz?'

'Ashalom.'

'I tell Ashalom he reminds me of one of those floating figures with a long trumpet William Blake draws, used to draw anyway; if you try to pull up and stop on a bridge he blows at you. Step there to the kitchen door, Walker, and tell Mrs. Littleberry to bring you a glass when she comes, she's fixing us some limeade, beautiful limes on the Keys.'

I was a little dazed with putting together how all this Highway shit tied into Schurz's anxiety and the sudden mention of Mrs. L was like coming out of the overcast with a view of the field. I said, 'Mrs. Littleberry?' as if I had never heard the name before. 'The cook?'

He said, 'Oh, she's everything. I never saw such a woman. Wonderful round the house. It's been a new place since she appeared.'

'Appeared, Uncle Nolan? Did she just *appear?*'

'Out of the blue, one of those things. You remember the little blow, not the last one, Flora I believe, or Ethel, no, Delia of course, why we named the cat, took up with us soon after.' (Delia was still up the palm tree.) 'The bus went on through to Miami but Mrs. Littleberry was apprehensive, got off. She asked at the gift shop if there was some place she could spend the night and Mrs. Maple, taking her for German I suppose (she's really Scandinavian I believe, 'Helga' might be either), put her in touch with Mrs. Schurz—who,' he smiled with his two bought teeth like scraps of white paper on a dingy floor, 'comes from Oklahoma. Schurz hardly speaks a word of German either. Odd the way things happen.'

I didn't like to tell him it might not be as odd as he thought, Schurz producing a quite possibly overseas cousin or what not to let her see what she could do with a rich and on-his-last-legs American widower, you hate to disillusion the old. I said I supposed she would be shoving off any time now, making a question of it, needing to find out, perhaps our worries were soon to be over, and he said helplessly, 'Where would she go, Walker? No children, no family, in a strange country.'

'In-laws?' I suggested. But he said the only one he knew of was the sister-in-law she had been staying with in Key West, who had been transferred, the husband had. 'Also, it seems there was some misunderstanding.' I said, 'About whose husband he was, ha-ha?' but Nolan doesn't take to such pleasantries. 'Married an Infantry officer in Munich, Navy maybe, who died on the way home——'

I said, 'Yes, yes,' before I could stop myself.

'Widow at thirty-three. What could be sadder?' I wanted
to say it might be sadder if she hadn't landed 'out of the blue'
on both feet like a surefooted heron but I didn't and he went
on, 'A godsend to me, Walker, quick, clean, smart, do anything, cut my hair the other day. And as a cook! I tell her
she plays the kitchen stove like a concert pianist. You'll see,
you *will* spend a few days?'

I thanked him, said I'd like to, went on to tell him about
everybody at home, how we tried to phone him but couldn't,
'worried about you and Gilda,' I felt like Stacy but I was
only trying to give it a lascivious twist for good-fellowship.
On the spur of the moment I said they had made me promise
to bring him back for a nice visit; it really seemed a brilliant
play-by-ear, get him back there where he could see the family,
see the fix we were in with *Beautiful Glenhaven,* renew old
family ties and affections, and particularly get him away
from Mrs. L for a while, not the hanky-panky that probably
went on, I don't know the cut-off age on that, but the very
good chance that Mrs. L had something more permanent in
mind.

He said there were certain difficulties, perhaps another
year, and I said, 'No time like the present, sir,' while I
swallowed ANOTHER YEAR and he said, 'The messages,
Walker, they're still coming in, I couldn't leave while they're
still coming in.'

I said Mrs. Littleberry could forward the mail. 'You'll
be back in a few weeks anyhow,' (I wanted it clear Mrs. L
wasn't in on the invitation).

He said with a kindly smile at my obtuseness, I didn't
understand, the messages didn't come by the U.S. Postal
Service he was pleased to say. Aside from which he had
promised Schurz to take Big Blue in the boat for a trial
flight over water. 'Big Blue's his number-one bird, we were
going last week but the wind wasn't right. Out to The Dry

Tortugas. I want to see Fort Jefferson, all in all Dr. Mudd is probably my favorite doctor.'

I didn't know at the time, who would? that Mudd was somehow connected with Lincoln's assassination (not why Nolan liked him though, not a sectional man) and I said if he was going that far to see a doctor wouldn't it be easier to talk to Dr. Arthur while he was at home? He laughed and said he wasn't planning to consult Dr. Mudd professionally, he felt fine, and we were back on that again and I was saying he looked fine, partly for the simple ingratiating content in the words and partly because I knew I didn't but largely because his health was so important to us and was naturally in the front of my mind, along with Mrs. L and Schurz and all the rest of it.

The only angle of it not perfectly obvious to anybody was Schurz's part in it, that is whether he was in business with Mrs. L on a kickback basis (he had produced her) or was just as naive as Nolan, practically as old, as if to prove you started out simple-minded and circled round to it again before you were through. In either case it seemed to me Mrs. L pretty well had it made—or would have had if we hadn't got there in time—the screen door behind me closing with a neat bump not the usual screen-door bang and Nolan saying in his model-T style, 'Come join us, Helga my dear, I was just introducing you to my young nephew. Mrs. Littleberry, Mr. Walker Bennett.'

'Williams, Uncle Nolan.'

'William Bennett, yes—that doesn't sound right, Walker.'

'Walker Williams, Uncle Nolan.'

He brushed it off with a laugh and 'Anyhow, my sister Iona's boy' (not his sister at all of course, his niece—the sort of thing that put Schurz on the phone I suppose).

She said, 'So?' hiding a natural dismay at the advent of kin, a woman of forty or thirty-five or forty-five, you never know, strong round arms and out-of-date 'shapely' legs (she wore a skirt that must have been the only one between Key West and Largo but she was feminine to begin with—I guessed she might have wanted a man but wouldn't under any circumstances want to be one). You hardly notice a woman's face any more but when I did I saw she was blond in that negligent matter-of-course German and Scandinavian way, Nolan going on with his antiquarian introduction about how 'Mrs. Littleberry had kindly consented' (kindly consented!) to move in and run his house for him, 'badly in need of a woman's touch.'

She said, 'Dear man!' to me with a caressing glance at Nolan, her tone a sort of reprimand for me as if I had denied it, setting down the tray and pitcher and accounting for the number of glasses with 'The Sergeant just called. I saw you had company and told him you had a young man with you but he said he'd be right over anyway. He's typed up everything in quintuplicate,' all with little or no accent. Then, 'Ach, sugar for the Sergeant!' disappearing for a minute or two and returning across the sand at a jog trot that seemed gawky in the flinging out of heels but less so in the joggling fronts, sugar in hand and spoons and a deprecating smile for Nolan's 'I was just saying, Helga, you've given the old man a new lease on life' (I wished Stacy had been there to help me hear it).

'Enough of "old"!' with a pouting smile.

'Well, I'm not exactly young.'

'I've seen men half your age who were older.'

He laughed, delighted. 'But you don't know my age,' basking in the intrinsic power words have, true or false.

'You're about sixty-three. I can tell. Fifty-nine, perhaps?'—as billing and cooing almost overwhelming.

Schurz broke it up before I got sick, zoomed in off the Highway and down the slope in a station wagon as long as

Queen Elizabeth II, the front end ducking with his stop, a puff of dust drifting forward round his hairy calves as he leaned back in and got a clipboard off the seat. Nolan started reminding him he knew Walker Bennett then got it right, smiling an apology to Mrs. L for names 'sometimes giving one trouble in the late fifties.'

Schurz manufactured enough surprise at the sight of me to have covered a resurrection but Nolan's eyes were on the clipboard (eye—you tended to forget only one was connected, except when you saw him at his arm-long telescope and everything seemed suddenly to jibe). 'I'm glad you brought it, Schurz, I want Walker to hear it. You'll agree with me, Walker, this is possibly the most astonishing thing since, well, I hardly know when, Joan of Arc's voices are roughly comparable but even that was different.'

Schurz gave me a solemn steady look while he was saying, 'I made five copies, Captain, like the old days,' and Nolan said with an exultant smile at me, 'The finest noncommissioned officer in the Service!' adding seriously to Schurz that he shouldn't have gone to all that trouble, there might be still more changes. 'Every time we run through it, Walker, things occur to me I overlooked mentioning, it's rather like those first pictures coming in bit by bit from the moon, a little one time, a little another. Make yourself comfortable, Schurz, and read Walker what we've got up to now. You needn't stay, my dear, you've heard it all,' whereupon 'my dear' poured limeade for everybody and skipped away at the jog trot (flung heels and this time the joggling rear) to no doubt do something with potato balls.

Nolan said to read it from the first, if I just heard some of it I wouldn't know where I was and Schurz gave his GI spectacles a stolid Teutonic going over with a khaki handkerchief, turned up yellow pages on the clipboard until he found what he wanted and began in a now-hear-this voice,

' "*FROM: Captain Nolan A. Bennett, F.A., U.S.A. TO: Whom it May Concern. SUBJECT: Captain Bennett's First Dream——*" '

'I did say dream, Schurz, but dream isn't right. I don't know what we ought to call it. Conference? Consultation? Appointment? Never mind, we'll straighten that out later. I couldn't distinguish much, Walker, not that it was dark— plenty of light, curtains against the sun—but much of the room, office really, with a sort of unresolved hazy quality, pre-decision, that reminded me of times in my old office in the History Building when I was puzzling how to grade a paper, roll-top desk, books, shelves, letter files, a few chairs, rather disorderly, table in the middle with a basket of fine peaches.'

I told him the peach season was over and he said, 'They might have been apples, Walker, like, you remember, '*The President has apples on the table and barefoot servants round him who adjust the curtains to a metaphysical t*,' it was that sort of place anyhow. People coming and going, not very distinct. I say people, that's confusing too but they seemed human enough, an old man at the desk, fine commanding beard, not a white man, not really black either, evidently a few north-European forebears way back. Ozias was standing just inside the door, a young man, tobacco colored, might have been an East-Indies boy or a Caloosa Indian, about Chak's height. Apparently Mr. C had been listening to some bulletins the boy had brought—they seemed to call him that, maybe C for Chancellor, or maybe there was a Mr. A and Mr. B somewhere higher up and Mr. C only super- intended one department, one galaxy' (I tried to catch Schurz's eye but he wouldn't look), 'anyway he seemed to have full authority in his district, and responsibility too be- cause he was fingering his forehead as if he had a headache coming on. I was there at the far end of the table in a chair much like this one but they didn't pay any attention to me, not at first I mean. He said, "Give me that again, son," and Ozias started reciting from memory.—Go on, Schurz, what did the boy say?'

Schurz found the place and began reading in the plodding matter-of-fact tone of going through Sick Report, glancing up now and then at the sea or the cove or the parachute palms or the interminable bridges of the Sunup-Sundown Highway, at anything, I thought, but me:

> *Ozias said, hands behind him, reciting, 'Two men walked into a candy store at 213 West 78th Street yesterday morning and asked for pumpkin pie. When the owner, Beno Spiewak, 61, told them there was only Danish pastry they shot him to death and critically wounded his wife——'*
>
> *'STOP!—No. go on.'*
>
> *'In another part of the city, when a hotel clerk, Simeon Miller, 44, accused a guest of causing a disturbance and asked him to leave, the guest shot him to death and at the main entrance, as he fled, shot to death the bellhop, Aston Foote, 71——'*
>
> *Mr. C banged on the table so hard one of the peaches rolled off the pile in the basket: 'How long shall I bear with this evil people that provoke me!' Then, when nobody moved or spoke with the shock of it and the room filled up and overflowed with silence, 'I think I'll just flush him out, Ozias. Flood the place again and wash him away.' 'Yes sir.' 'Or blow him away! I've got squalls growing up could scatter him like the chaff which the wind driveth away. He doesn't believe I can do it, hasn't seen it so he doesn't believe it, wouldn't believe he has a nose on his face if I didn't let him cross his eyes and see it.'*

Ozias said there was no question he could do it and Mr. C said, 'He thinks it's a wind when we let it out to a hundred miles an hour. Why, he's never had any real wind, Ozias. We could sweep him up like powdered dung and cast him a thousand miles into outer darkness.'

'Oh, yes sir.'

'Or visit him with fiery serpents and burn him up, it doesn't matter how we do it, one way or another destroy him from the face of the earth. It repents me I ever put him there. Every imagination of the thoughts of his heart is only evil continually. Sit down, son, I need somebody to talk to, it's always lonesome in the Front Office,' drumming on the table while Ozias replaced the peach and sat down uncomfortably as if the chair were damp. 'Things are not right down there, Ozias, we might as well face it. What you tell me is bad enough but there's worse. I don't mean this moon business, this cruising round a little out in the Galaxy, I mean him to have some curiosity; we can take care of that, knock those things down any old time. And I don't mean this big-explosion trick he's stumbled on, though at his stage it's like a five-year-old meddling in his father's desk and coming on a loaded pistol. What worries me—and makes me angry too though I know I oughtn't to get angry——'

'You oughtn't to let little things down there bother you, sir, it's not worth it.'

'Sometimes, Ozias, I get so mad——Lot stopped in to see me the other day, too polite to say so but I could tell he didn't think I was doing right to sit back and let these people go on the way they're going, doing right by Sodom I mean, they have thousands of cities the equal of Sodom. I had to admit I might have lost

*my temper with Sodom, been hasty. One thing is sure
though, son, I was either hasty then or I'm way over-
patient now—but I was saying something else.'*

*'You were saying what worried you. Is it something
special, sir, or just the whole toot and scramble?'*

'Yes. What worries me . . .'

Schurz was slow lifting a page and I broke in to say, 'My
God, Uncle No, what did you have for supper!' I thought
he would laugh or smile or say something about Mrs. L's
cooking but he only looked at me as you might look at a
strange dog with no collar that has showed up in the yard,
saying nothing and after a second signaling Schurz to continue.

*'. . . worries me is that after all this time they haven't
got any better sense than to cast away the best thing I
gave them. I told them to be fruitful and multiply but
I didn't mean just turn out more and more* bodies. *The
idea was to breed souls, breed spirit, the only reason I
put them there in the first place.'*

'The Experiment, yes sir.'

*'Whatever you want to call it. I don't much like giving
it a name, you name something too soon and you cut
down its potentials, it might want to be something else
with another name. And it wasn't just right, I know
that. But it was shaping up, a good beginning, had gone
along far enough to give it a try, you have to test out
these things under actual conditions, you know, dry run,
shakedown cruise. Anyhow, I had put a lot of time and
thought on it. They were supposed to do their part,
take care of it, cultivate it, help it to grow. And of
course at times some of them did, a few. It has always
had its ups and downs but there have usually been
enough sagacious people to watch over it, people who*

knew what I was driving at, thought *they knew, important people able to set an example—Moses, Mohammed, Gautama, Kung—people who realized the brain was a good thing as far as it went but it wasn't meant to handle everything, people who left room in their figuring for the things you can't see straight on, see only if you look a little to one side, close one eye. I put in a good strong brain to help him get something to eat, a place to sleep, cover his skin as the hair wore off, get comfortable enough to develop this other thing in peace and quiet. I didn't mean get comfortable so he could have more time for fighting and fornication, for just being an animal. I've got plenty of animals, no problem about that.'*

'No sir.'

'The problem was to see if I couldn't take one *animal and lift him up to a new level. If I could then I figured I'd go back and bring up another one. One by one until two or three or four of them got up where they could get some idea of the situation. I was afraid to try it with all of them at once——'*

'I understand, sir.'

'Too much of a risk, Ozias. If I had miscalculated— and it's beginning to look now as if that's just what I did—I might have to destroy everything, the way I was tempted to do with some ice back there fifteen or twenty thousand years ago, I forget when it was. I can't remember what stopped me.'

'It's not likely you miscalculated, sir.'

'Oh, I miscalculate all the time, boy, I'm not a wizard. I think I may have miscalculated on the generator somewhere, may be running too much current through there for the size of the fiber. They're always overheating, blowing fuses, setting things on fire.'

'*Yes sir, but—but——*'

'*But what? Don't mind speaking out, Ozias, I want to know what you think. You don't think it's the generator?*'

'*It works fine with simple forms, sir, they generate fine, never have any trouble. I'd say the generator was foolproof.*'

'*You're thinking it's something else then?*'

'*Well, sir, I look at it this way, they're the only ones give you any trouble and they're the ones you put the Experiment in, I'm wondering if the Experiment is the thing overloads. . . .*'

I couldn't help cutting in to say it sounded like Mollenbrink trying to put a Porsche engine in his Volkswagen. 'The engine went in all right but the tires were too small, the brakes weren't strong enough, the battery was too weak, and he couldn't get at the valves,' my laugh crackling into the laughlessness like a burglar falling down stairs, jokes never cross the Gap.

Nolan ignored it, maybe he didn't see the point, motor cars nothing in his life (the one Aunt Mat drove them to Pelican in was parked right over there beyond Schurz's battlewagon), particularly the insides. His only response was to hold out a just-a-minute hand to Schurz: 'There's something back in there I overlooked, Schurz; about his wondering if it wouldn't have been better if he had put the Experiment in one of the quadrupeds, tigers maybe, maybe dogs, made them the human animal. Or adapted it a little here and there and put it in one of the plants, they didn't move round so much, had more time to take care of it. Or one of the birds. Never mind, we'll make another insert. And we ought to mention too there were people coming and going during all this, reporting on this and that, wanting him to sign things, marchers beyond the window, Sodomites demanding reparations somebody said, a few noisy Romans among them protesting he had brought down the Empire for less than the USA was getting away with scot-free. One boy came in to report picking up a Chinese communist trying to infiltrate one of the gym classes, they thought he was a spy, he said the Presbyterian missionaries had showed him how to get up there. Mr. C said he was busy worrying now, he'd talk to him after a while.—We'll put it in later, go on.'

'. . . overloads them.'

'It might be, son, I suppose it might be. In any case it's too late to worry about that now. My worry is, do I salvage what I can? (I tried that with Noah, you remember, and look what's happened), or do I just smash the whole thing and start over again farther out in the Galaxy? Or in another galaxy, why not? I've got the space.'

'You've got plenty of room, sir.'

'Because one thing for sure, Ozias, we can't go on this way. If they can't handle it, or won't—this thing I gave them, singled them out and gave them, this Medal of Honor (unmerited)—I'll have to make other arrangements, which will take a little time. It won't do to have them throw it away before I've arranged where to put it, I mean they could paint us into a very tight corner.'

'I don't see what harm they can do to us.'

'It's too complicated to go into all of it with you right now.'

'I'd say if they want to be animals so bad just let them go ahead and be animals—sir.'

'Yes, well that's all right if I've got time to break in another one. It wouldn't take too long with some of *the fish but I've got to know beforehand. You can see how those things are already reflecting up here, I can't sit and let it all build up into another Rebellion, one Black Sheep is a gracious plenty. Much as I'd hate to destroy him after all the work and worry I've put on him I don't see how I can take the risk of not doing it; if I don't destroy him he may well destroy us.'*

'Preemptive Strike, sir?'

'Sometimes I think I took him up out of the water too soon, should have left him in that rich oceanic broth I'd boiled up until he got more like a porpoise then eased him out—spilt milk! What were we saying?'

'You were talking about calling him in, sir.'

'Not calling him in, I don't want him up here, burning the files, defecating on the floor, arguing about everything. Canceling him out, that's what I mean. And I've been thinking a good day to do it would be one of the great holy days he has desecrated, hasn't had imagination enough to respect, Christmas might be a good day.'

'You wouldn't have to wait till Christmas, sir, just muscle up one of the winds——'

'Christmas morning, say, about ten o'clock. What month is it today, Ozias? I lose track of time there's been so much of it.' Ozias said it was September and the old man said, 'I don't mean that calendar, I like the Aztec one better, are you trying to say something, Nolan?'

Captain Bennett struggled to his feet and moved round closer hand by hand on the table to supplement his shaking knees. He hardly recognized his own voice when he heard it saying, 'Excuse me, sir, for interrupting but——'

'Go on.'

'Things may not be as bad down there as you think. The newspapers and television, sir, have to make things look as bad as possible to stay in business——'

'This is Nolan Bennett, isn't it?'

'Yes sir.'

'Saw your grandfather the other day, Nolan, looking well. I was teasing him about how he wouldn't believe me when I told him to make an offer on that bottom land while it was under water and nobody wanted it. I said, 'Go ahead, it may come in handy one day'—I like swamp land and lagoons, reminds me of the old days . . .'

And I couldn't help interrupting, myself. I said, 'Excuse me, Uncle Nolan, sir, but didn't you think it was peculiar for everybody to be speaking English, I mean, after all, wouldn't you think, well, Hebrew maybe?' (just to draw him down out of the clouds a mile or two, wind him in like a kite).

Which it didn't do. 'It came through to *me* in English, Walker,' (trying to put it in words of one syllable). 'Quite possibly by some method of instantaneous translation, you have a crude form of it at the United Nations I understand. No, nothing strange about the language, it was the words, the meaning. What he was saying, Walker, or seemed to be, as I get it, was there's some sort of give-and-take about this business, some back-and-forth tie-in, some sort of reciprocal generation you might say, a discovering outward that discovers inward, as a poet may be said to write the poem while it is writing him, as one is ennobled by his deed of imagining nobly—we don't really have the thoughts for it yet.'

There was too much money in the pot for me to let go our regular kick-out 'Shit!' and I settled for saying I wondered if that Chinese boy, used to puzzles, could puzzle it out. He said it was easier to understand if you didn't think about it, thought a little to one side of it, looking off at the glittering Ocean or Gulf or Straits or whatever it was and tossing in, 'Outer winds, Walker, continue to bring in faint persistent signals the world of reason is not the whole structure.'

I glanced at Schurz but he was studying some sky way over my head. I said, 'ESP, Uncle Nolan?' (I couldn't be sure how seriously he took all this).

'ESP?'

'Or UFO?'

He said he couldn't keep up with all these alphabet words and I said, 'Unidentified Flying Objects?'

He brushed it off with a sweep of his hand and 'Oh, he wouldn't go about it in such a vulgar way!—I told him as politely as I could there were thousands of people down here who valued this "difference" he was talking about, this "Experiment," this spirit that made them human. And I said even if it turned out there was only *one* thousand he wouldn't want to destroy them with the others.—Go on, Schurz, what did he say?'

> He smiled at Ozias and then at Captain Bennett, a wry sort of smile, and said, 'I know that one, Nolan.'
>
> 'How do you mean, sir?'
>
> 'I say, "No, not if there are a thousand." And you say, "Peradventure there be only nine hundred?" Abraham used that on me with Sodom.'
>
> 'Well, sir, I hadn't——'
>
> 'And when we looked into it he could only produce one man. One man, Nolan!'
>
> Captain Bennett said, 'Yes sir, but *you* looked into it. That's what I mean. With all respect, sir, don't you

think you could look into it again before you decide anything, the way you did that time?'

Mr. C twisted some strands of beard round his first finger then said things were very different up there now, as he had been telling Ozias. 'Everybody thinks he wants to be free; make them free and they say, "Nobody loves us, we're lonesome." Liberate these people, Nolan, and they go crazy. They're like a kite when you let go the string, it's only pulling against the string keeps them up. It used to be I could tell a man to come and he would come, do this and he would do it. Now I have to consult him, discuss it, talk about his rights, listen to why some other way of doing it would be better, why this? why that? and by that time it's too late to do it. There's so much talk nowadays, Nolan! So many words on the road, in the air. No wonder there're jams and collisions. If everybody would just keep his mouth shut for ten days you wouldn't know the place,' breathing a sigh that trembled the fringe of his moustache and going on that it would be next to impossible to find anybody willing to go down there. 'Nobody wants that sort of work any more. The two boys I sent to Sodom had a very rough time of it, you know, people rioting, demonstrating, picketing Lot's house who had kindly taken them in, throwing stones. Everybody I've ever sent down there has been subjected to indignities of one kind or another. I really don't like to ask somebody to go through it again.'

Captain Bennett told him that what some envoy might have to go through wouldn't be as rough as what the thousand would have to bear being destroyed off the face of the earth and he admitted that. 'But it's hard to deal with people, Nolan, unless they have some values because you can't tell where to put the pressure.

These people don't value anything except fornication and money. And talk, yes, talk. I overheard one of them saying just the other day, "Life is of no value but suicide is futile because death doesn't matter either."'

'We say a lot of things we don't really mean.'

'Oh, I'm aware of that, I make allowances for that.'

'You take my own kin people, sir—not to ask any special privileges, you understand, special treatment—honest, hardworking, moral, upright——'

'No doubt, Nolan, no doubt, I haven't checked them out lately. But sending somebody, I'll have to think about it, I just don't know.' He asked Ozias if he knew anybody among the young men who might volunteer to go and Ozias said not offhand he didn't. 'Ask around among your friends, Ozias. Say it oughtn't to be as bad a trip as the others, a different kind of mission, purely for reconnaissance, keeping his eyes open and his mouth shut, not making the police mad with him talking too much, feeding crowds in unusual ways, curing the sick and making the doctors mad, reviving the dead, that sort of thing confuses everybody. I'd want him to learn everything he could in a short time consistent with getting back whole, not stabbed and stoned and suffering from shock, I don't want that. I don't know, Nolan, it's really too much to ask of anybody . . . .'

Schurz said he had a note at that point things were beginning to (thank God) fade out and it reminded me of Nolan's scheme he had told us about once of putting dreams on film and I made the mistake of saying, 'My God, Uncle No, if you'd just had your camera!'—I thought it was high time we had a laugh.

Which we didn't get. He said that brought back something he had overlooked if Schurz would be kind enough to work it in. 'He said to me at one stage, "Now something else, Nolan, as long as you're up here. That business you've been digging into—*hallucinema*, if you want the name—are you getting anywhere?" (of course he knew I wasn't). I told him it was slow but I wasn't discouraged and he said, "I'm holding out some parts on you, Nolan, to be frank about it. The truth is I don't much like the idea right now. You see, I've been careful to give everything two sides, things stand up better that way, sometimes more but at least two, and to let you come along now with pictures that would do away with the dark side, turning them inside out like that, when we both know they don't get along any too well as it is—it makes me wonder, Nolan, if you've been listening to the Big Talker, the one I threw out of here, well, never mind, that's a large subject and it's getting late——" '

'And I'm out of cigarettes,' I cut in with, slapping my pockets as if I might come on some spares. I had heard enough. Much more than enough to understand Schurz's phoning the family (or the Coast Guard, indeed), but enough to set me thinking I'd better grab a phone too and get a refill from Stacy— whose first question would be, What does the doctor say? or maybe, How long has he got? and I knew I needed to have a talk with Schurz, if I could get some privacy. There was no indication he had called a doctor but if he had I needed to know what had happened, and if he hadn't (waiting until I came, or Nolan refusing to see anybody but Dr. Mudd) the best thing seemed clearly to take Nolan home and have Dr. Arthur look at him, *listen* to him, he looked all right. I said to Schurz, preparing a wink in case he didn't get it, that maybe he wouldn't mind running me up to the Gift Shop, they would have cigarettes.

Before he could say anything Nolan had lifted his brown-spotted hand at me. 'Just a minute, Walker, there was another message, hardly more than a flash and I can't say whether it was on my first trip there or another trip, probably later because he had wanted a little time to think about it, anyway it couldn't be more important, about sending somebody, what did he say, Schurz?'

'Yes sir, he said—let's see, let's see, here it is. He said,

> *'I rigged up for you a sort of hollow sphere, Nolan. I put in everything you could possibly use for a long time, matter, energy, space, even time itself, nothing outside of the sphere, not even nothing.'*
> *'You, sir.'*
> *'No, I'm in there too, I put everything in——'*

Nolan stopped him with, 'No, no, Schurz, that's not the one, I mean the one about sending somebody.'

'Oh yes, yes.—Yes, here we are.'

> *He said, 'I'm going to do what you ask, Nolan—if I can lay my hands on somebody.'*
> *'You're going to look into it, sir!'*
> *'To satisfy you, and to satisfy myself too whether they have done altogether to the cry of it which is come unto me. If I did it for Abraham——'*
> *Captain Bennett thanked him, tears of gratitude running down into his beard and Mr. C said, 'If I did it for Abraham it's only fair to do it for you . . . .'*

'Do you hear that, Walker!'

'He's sending a serviceman, yes sir.' (I could hardly stand it; it reminded me of babysitting with Sisterbaby when she was five, having to play slapjack with her until I was ready to throw up.)

'I thanked him again. I was so pleased I couldn't help a little banter and I said I thanked him a thousand times, which brought a smile to his face. I said to send the boy straight to me I'd take care of everything, put him up, show him around, give him every possible cooperation. (I didn't say so, Walker, but I thought I'd send him up home first thing, let him meet you all, start him out with the right impression, not trying to pull any strings you understand just letting him see for himself.) I said I'd take care of his expenses, not to bother about that, I said, "That bottom land you helped Grandfather to buy, sir, it's worth ten times what it was then, twenty times, and I'll sell off whatever is necessary to cover any costs may arise——" '

'Bottom land!' I could hardly find breath to say it.

'It's quite a large tract on the river, Walker, as you're probably too young to remember.'

I said, 'Now, Uncle Nolan,' and ran out of words, the damp Gulf-Stream wind mixing the sweat on my lips into a sort of paper-hanger's paste that made it hard to say anything. 'You wouldn't need to sell—they wouldn't send him down here flat broke without any money, Uncle Nolan.'

'And of course I can realize a substantial amount on The Home Place alone, the few acres adjacent to Stacy's abomination.'

'He'd have credit cards, Uncle Nolan, would certainly be on an expense account. You won't have to sell any land, just show him around, introduce him, show him where everything is, that sort of thing,' realizing all at once I was accepting the whole nutsy business on . Nolan's terms and pulling out by reminding him, 'In any case you won't have to sell anything until he gets here.'

He said he wasn't thinking so much of the boy's everyday expenditures. 'I'm thinking of what we'll have to do on our own. Even if he goes back and gets a stay we can't expect it to be anything but short, a year or two maybe, to give us a fighting chance to right things, make a real effort, show we mean it, show we've got it in us (if we have, I sometimes wonder). It'll take quite a sum to get all that in operation, I haven't worked out the details, I'll want to talk to lots of different people—poets, artists, astronomers, musicians, inventors—then I'll want to talk to a lawyer, Helga knows a lawyer in Key West, helped her with her papers.'

I said, Wouldn't he rather talk to Mr. Cuyler at home, knew his affairs, drew his will? swallowing, the word always made me swallow, (Addison Cuyler, Secrest, Weeks, Swicegood & Barnes—Addison was only about seventy-nine). But he was on a different tack now. 'Fortunately all of you at home, Walker, are well provided for, and fortunately my dear friend sitting over there has everything he can possibly want——'

'You'll plant me anyhow, Captain,' Schurz said politely.

'I'll set something aside to make sure Helga is well taken care of, but beyond that I have no obligations.'

It was like listening to the tube sexing up Hurricane Gilda except we hadn't been in her path, this calamity was slashing and clawing straight at us. I said, 'Uncle Nolan——'

'I know what you're going to say, Walker. You think this is hasty of me after so few talks up there' (I wished for Stacy—to share the persecution but also to hear it all for himself, which he wasn't going to believe when I had to tell him and was somehow at the same time going to hold me responsible for) 'but the truth is I've been thinking along these lines for many months. Mr. C practically took the words out of my mouth. What do we see reading back over the diary we keep in the daily press but crime, corruption, riots, drugs, obscenity, air-and-water pollution yes, but mind pollution as well, soil erosion that reads like a misprint for soul erosion . . .' on and on, the usual antiquated gripes of his contemporary fossils. 'We have made scabrous words romantic and noble words unspeakable, made it less shameful to converse of bodily functions than of patience, integrity, discipline. The only word that shocks us is *censorship*, yet any guard is a censor, any thou-shalt-not, any traffic light that goes red, every movement of the bowels is a censorship but it is impolite to discuss anything beyond the movement it-self——'

'Uncle Nolan——'

'Stupidity, head-in-the-sandism. We wouldn't need to build a single motor car for five years and we're going to build fifty million . . .'

I cut off in there somewhere to think about the barrels of this gun we were standing in front of, about the Private Eye on the way down, the Agent, about how long it would take him to make the trip, how long we had, all of it jumbled together under a coating of Keys-sweat.

And cut back in too soon: 'There are problems that need to be solved, that we know the solutions for and that if solved would shed new light on problems we *don't* know the solutions for, but do we solve them? We'd rather talk about the ones we can't solve. How do you go at solving a big problem, Walker?'

I said I wished (to Christ) I knew and he said, 'First you peel it, trim off all the outside details that are not problematical. This leaves you with the big problem encased now with semi-problems, that is, problems you know how to solve but haven't got round to solving yet. Next you solve the semi-problems, one by one—any dog knows you chase one rabbit at a time—which leaves the big problem bare where you can see it. Chances are there is now an outside layer of *new* semi-problems you hadn't seen before and you peel them off one by one. All the time the big problem is getting smaller, getting more manageable——'

I broke in to say I thought he had told Mr. C things weren't as bad down here as they looked and he threw in 'The more people the less freedom,' like an outboard giving an extra cough after the ignition is cut, adding in a quieter voice, 'Yes, I wasn't being quite on the level with him, Walker, but there was—is—so much at stake. And he didn't seem to hold it against Abraham. And also, Walker, I was thinking of the longer span, of things we have now and take for granted that required centuries to grow, most of the kindnesses are new, many of the restraints. An old father of five sons asked Xerxes if he would leave the eldest to care for him, take the other four on the invasion of Greece but leave one. It annoyed the King and he had the father's body cut asunder and placed to the right and left of the Great Road so the Army could march out between them——'

I knocked over my glass of limeade but it didn't shake him.

'A citizen gave advice to the Athenians that angered them and they stoned him to death; and when the women learned of it they flocked to his house and stoned to death his wife and his children. We don't behave like that now. A horse threw his rider, who had grooms take the animal to the spot and cut off his four legs at the hock——'

'Uncle Nolan——'

'Good is in the lead, a faster grower over the centuries than evil.'

I sprang into the breath-pause to say I thought it would work out all right because the agent Mr. C was sending would have his own questionnaire, would turn in his own report, and Schurz—who had been sitting without word or motion, letting me see for myself I suppose, hear for myself— seized on the brief silence to suggest I might care to drive round a bit before lunch, leaning over his bare knees as if making himself lighter, ruffling the pages like little wings.

I said I certainly would, trying to get up with a seemly reluctance, while Nolan was saying good-naturedly, 'You can't drive round on the Keys, Schurz, you go one way or the other.'

I winced at Schurz's 'You'll come along won't you, Captain?' though it sounded as hollow as a beached shell. But Nolan said for us 'boys' to go on without him. 'Leave me the script, there may be something else I overlooked and I'd better write it in while it's fresh in my mind, I sometimes think my memory's not what it used to be,' Schurz and I scrambling over each other to reach the getaway car.

He called after us, If we saw Delia up there waiting for the mail to please tell her he wanted to see her, and Schurz said, 'Will do,' (we didn't see her, didn't look very hard).

3

AS HE SWUNG US sunup on the Highway I asked him how far it was to the closest bottle of whisky, my throat tight and the words sounding as if I had the croup.

There is no use getting mad with somebody who has his right foot in the bin and his left in the grave or the other way round but sometimes you can't help it, the grave (or bin) yawning, as the expression goes, in his face while the rest of us had the future before us, or would have had, where all this left it was anybody's guess. Of course none of us had seen the will but he gave every indication of having a normal and decent affection for his kin people and it was certainly reasonable to suppose he would do the right thing, or would have if old C had kept his nose out of it; true the 'something' he might set aside for Mrs. L wouldn't be as bad as what she would pocket as Mrs. N. Bennett, but the rest of his proposal could easily wipe out every nickel in the Folly land and The Home Place too, not counting lawyers' fees—destroy us off the face of the earth indeed, us caught in a sort of double pocket where if Mr. C didn't get us Nolan would (according to Nolan's nightmare I mean), a prospect really too ugly to look at, Stacy somehow, I didn't doubt, blaming me for the ugliness and retaliating in who could foresee what underhanded ways, de-nepotizing me (whether there's such a word or not) out of my job (my 'partnership') for one simple example, ripping off my epaulets, my private-first-class stripe. 'Is he on acid, Mr. Schurz?' 'Acid?' 'Acid, speed, grass. Does he sniff? Does he smoke pot?' 'Never had a cigar in his life'—sometimes the Gap gives you the feeling you've been captured by aborigines.

Stacy was disagreeable, not just bad news but bad news collect. And bad news he had to work to decode on account of Mrs. Maple there fumbling and dusting and rearranging her pennants and postcards and pillows and pecans that were close by to give her a wiretap on the naked wall-phone (Schurz parked outside, maneuvering trying to get each piece of the car into a patch of gusty clacking shade like somebody tucking a blanket round him on a January night). I told Stacy there was a little static on the line but he didn't get the point and I tried some other double talk about the barometer down there being lower than we had expected and predicted to go still lower, Mrs. Maple frowning at the one behind the cash register while I puzzled my brain for a different code, Stacy squawking he didn't give a damn what the weather was, if I was trying to break the news Nolan was folding just hand it to him straight he was man enough to take it.

I told him, No, the property I had come to look at was apparently sound, 'Heart pine and cypress,' I said, 'no termites anywhere that I can see'—it wasn't getting through and I tried to be more specific by saying it was generally in good repair except there were a few leaks in the second story. 'Some bats have definitely got into the attic,' I said, 'and they're breeding.' 'Doing what!' I said breeding other bats and dropped it, too complicated. I told him the worst part was that there were going to be other bids on the property and also there might be less acreage in the piece than we had been figuring on.

His first response was to say hang up and find a phone I could talk sense over but he must have been getting enough of it not to want to suffer another collect call because he changed his mind and said he had better come down there himself if I couldn't handle it (consolidating the blame where he could lay hands on it), knew all along he should have attended to it himself. He said to get him a room at the motel, there *was* a motel?

I said a couple of bridges down, the *Ship-n-Shore*, and he said, 'I'm wondering, Walker, if I hadn't better bring Mollenbrink much as I hate the idea. Here's my thinking on that' (as if showing me a Diner's Card), 'if the old bastard should really get the bugs and rewrite the will we'll want to have somebody like Leon we can put on the stand as to his mental condition, or if it's best for his own good to let him go off to a sanatorium for a spell—yes, I better bring Leon, get two rooms, Walker, I don't want the son of a bitch watching my dreams, just a minute, Walker, just a minute, I better find out what sort of bill he'd be throwing at us, not to lead him into temptation with a blank check, get *one* room.' 'For when, Stacy? You coming tonight?' He said he couldn't leave today, Livonia had some scheme she wanted to talk to him and Mamma about when he got home from the salt mine. 'Tomorrow, Walker—well, this is my nickel' (he never misses) and that ended it.

Schurz drove us across a few of those interminable low-lying bridges that almost make you seasick, gulls tailing us as if we had been a shrimp boat. At the *Red Man's Bar & Grill* which doubled as eatery for the *Ship-n-Shore* Schurz ordered a beer (and poured it as solicitously as if he had been back in Milwaukee and brewed it himself) and I put a little water in my whisky in the light of my possibly already murky image and drank it down.

While it was spreading its nourishment through my open-mouthed veins like plant food through one of Mamma's dried-out begonias I tried to add up where we were and what I could lead Mr. Schurz into doing for us; what Nolan could do for (and to) us—and clearly might do—was obviously deadly. Though I thought we could persuade him to hold off selling any property until the Agent actually landed, which at least would delay it, still during the delay Mrs. L might well be joining the family, *becoming* the family as far as inheritance was concerned, 'surviving spouse' up her sleeve like a gravity knife. I said, trying to open Schurz up with the first oyster-knife came to hand, 'Mrs. Littleberry seems to know a good pad when she hits one,' the beer in front of him like a crystal ball and him reading it. He said in a minute, rather close to the chest I thought, 'She thinks the world of the Captain.'

'I gathered that but——'

'They all love the Captain. I remember once outside of Angoulême——'

I said I didn't mean was she fucking the Captain? (he jumped as if he hadn't heard the word since the Armistice)

I meant what was she up to for the long pull? I meant did she *have designs* on the Captain? hoping that was sufficiently antique to reach him but adding 'Wedding bells, Mr. Schurz?' in case it wasn't. He shook his head as if I had asked him to predict the names of next year's hurricanes but went far enough to say the Captain had his head on the ground, feet on his shoulders he meant, and I said that was exactly what worried me. 'Do you think he really has? I think we ought to get him to a doctor, Mr. Schurz.' He said there were a lot of doctors not as smart as the Captain, and I went back to puzzling whether Mr. Schurz was dumb or didn't trust me (he kept on failing to look at my denim eye) or whether he was really backing Mrs. L, having produced her.

A sudden whiskied panic struck me—I was still weak from the widow—that Nolan might already have used his Lifetime Exemption on Mrs. L and I said, feeling my way, that if I were the Captain I'd certainly hand somebody a nice little tax-free package of thirty Gs; 'I'd hate for the undertaker to catch me with my Exemption hanging out.' But Schurz didn't know anything, or wouldn't tell. He said, 'The dreams are what's bothering him, Mr. Bennett,' and I said, 'Williams,' and he said, 'How's he going to show the man around without letting him see too much?'

'The man?'

'The Agent, Mr. Bennett.'

It rocked you. I told him I'd give the Captain a mouthful of my sleeping pills tonight, a good nightmareless night's sleep and maybe 'the man' wouldn't show up. He said, 'The Captain never takes pills, says that's why he's not sick,' and I came back to calling a doctor: 'Anybody swallows all that dreamshit can use a doctor.'

He drank a little beer then a little more and I thought he wasn't going to answer, then he said, 'Well, you take my pigeons, Mr. Bennett. If somebody just grabbed you and

56

took you off five hundred miles and set you out on a country road in the middle of nowhere and told you to go on back home you would ramble around trying to find somebody to tell you where you were and somebody who would hitch you to a bus stop and somebody who could tell you about bus connections——'

'And whether I wanted to go home anyhow.'

'—you would fool away half a day waiting for the bus and getting started, and then you would only get back home because there was a bus and the bus driver knew the road and showed you the way. My pigeons just go up and take one look-around and head out for home. I mean we can't understand that. And the Captain he figures there are a lot of other things—that porpoise lounging round the dock, Captain says he's got a bigger brain than yours or mine or his, maybe we don't get signals old porpoise gets all the time.'

I signaled I was giving up by throwing back the last of my whisky.

When Nolan went for his nap, after a lunch of Mrs. L's luscious weltwienergestaltbraten or whatever it was, a brief interlude took place in the continuity of our deteriorating relationship that almost loosed my bowels, demoralized already from a sleepless night, Mrs. L tapping a finger on her lips as Nolan disappeared and kicking off her shoes. She pointed two or three times at mine, me stammering over the unexpectedness of it, the catastrophe of it, such an invitation in my pulverized state, stammering in a search for some ruttish way of saying Drained! that wouldn't imply the proposal terrified me, which it did. My eyeballs seemed to have threads fastened to them at the back with little weights attached to the threads, seemed ready to slide down behind my face if I didn't squint, my left shoulder was still almost useless from the poundings the widow had given it in her frenzies, and as for the thing itself it felt as boned and shapeless as ground round. I was afraid to put her off with 'Tomorrow' (it always infuriates them) but there was at the moment nothing in life I wanted less than what Mrs. L indicated she had in mind—not that it was out of character, (we laugh at the old saying that the way to a man's heart is through his stomach—'heart!'—but there's more to it than meets the hasty ear, with a cooking woman apt to be resourceful and inventive and imaginative and clean and interested and pleased at the dish whether she's vertical or horizontal). But the simple truth was I was in no shape for Mrs. L and knew it; even my shoe laces seemed to know it, twisting into knots as I tried to untie them.

Then it was over. She may have noticed something half-hearted in the way I couldn't find the tab of my zipper, or she may have come on a sudden suspicion I might be a plant the family had sent in there to trap her, spoil her bid for 'surviving spouse,' in any case she abruptly whispered, 'Everyone quiet as a mouse while he takes his nap, maybe another message, who knows?' gliding away with dishes as velvet-pawed as the absent cat. 'I'll dry,' I said, happy enough to have mopped the linoleum ('dry' on my mind I reckon), but she wouldn't have it, shutting herself in the kitchen without a sound—leaving me wondering if, on second thought, I couldn't manage later today, her shape lingering in my eyes like a photographer's flashbulb.

When Nolan appeared again he looked refreshed, replenished, almost redecorated, with damp white hair brushed back over ears like the wings of a sitting tern, and at the same time uncertain and puzzled as if his mind wasn't altogether easy, or what was left of it. He beckoned us away from the house, Schurz and me, with a conspiratorial tilt of the head, saying nothing until he had halted near the dock and sat down on the salt-bleached pink bottom of an overturned rowboat. (Schurz had zoomed over to Oyster for a bite of lunch—and maybe an old-man's snooze—and zoomed back as Nolan emerged from the house, as if they operated on synchronized watches). We sat beside him. I don't know what Schurz expected, maybe he had been round the place long enough to be ready for anything; I braced myself for an afternoon version of a new nightmare, a nap-mare, wondering if Stacy would okay a General-wear-and-tear entry on my expense account.

'Something has begun to dawn on me, Schurz. I don't know how to put this without you both thinking I've lost my mind.'

Schurz said, 'Oh Captain!' with his hollow-shell laugh and I said, 'Oh Uncle Nolan!' with mine, and he said after a precautionary glance over shoulder, 'About Helga, I mean,' giving me the sickening thought I was about to hear of the dawn of superannuated love, the dawn of Mrs. L as heiress.

'She's been a godsend to me, Schurz, you've heard me say so the odd time.'

'Oh yes sir.'

'But I'm just now understanding this term that's been put in my mouth. What started it was—while I was lying down a few minutes ago a bit of the meeting came back to me I'd forgotten. Mr. C, you remember, was talking about how hard it would be to find anyone willing to make the trip down here nowadays: "You can't just appoint somebody any more, you've got to consult him, listen to him, discuss it, argue about it——" '

'Yes sir, we've got that.'

'But I'd forgotten what Ozias said—some day I'm going to forget my shirt. Ozias asked him if he had ever thought of trying to get a woman to do it. Ozias said, "The male, sir, is no better than he used to be, if as good, but the *female*," smiling at me (incidentally an amusing boy), "she can do everything but change a tire." He reminded the old man that modern American hurricanes were all female, but they were bringing in the young Chinese for questioning and things were clouding over. But, Walker——'

My face muscles had been pulling in two or three different directions for several seconds but I thought my voice sounded cool and fairly everyday; I said, 'I don't see how she could be the one, Uncle Nolan, because——'

'Her very name, Walker! Helga, holy.'

'—because she was here a week or two, month or two, before you asked him to send somebody' (here cooking up the pigs' knuckles and sauerbraten and dulieberschnitzel-bankwürstchen that made you ask him I couldn't quite say).

'I thought of that, Walker, but you can't go by that. Time's a very tricky invention at best—apparently running only one way, which is obviously impossible, leading you to the simple explanation that we're not yet sharp enough to get the whole story, as primitive people are said to have trouble understanding how the river gets back into the mountains to run again. Or possibly it's tide-like—"time and tide," —flowing out then flowing in, drawn by the phases of who can say what; we're not quite up to it yet. Quite possibly the meeting up there the other night was a rerun of a visit I made months ago and forgot, maybe years ago. I noticed as I talked to them I had no feeling of being an old man though I *am* getting along, felt quite young in fact. Maybe I was.'

I let that go, searching for something concrete that would get Mrs. L back on the ground with the rest of us and coming up with the question of credentials. I said, 'Does she have any sort of ID, Uncle Nolan? Passport? letter of introduction? driver's license? you know what I mean, they would have given her something in case she got in trouble.'

'Not necessarily, Walker. The two boys he sent to Sodom didn't have any letter of introduction that I ever heard of, any "driver's license." There are things you have to take on faith.'

'Has she *said* anything? I mean, does she claim she is——'

'Walker,' he laughed, 'you talk like a Godless Roman soldier in Palestine! She makes no claim at all, quite likely for the very good reason she knows nothing about it. A person doesn't know much about what he really is, what makes him think and feel the way he does, why he likes shrimp one day and crab another. I don't mean she has bodily come down to earth like an aeroplane, I'm not in my dotage, I mean that at some time after the meeting, the original meeting, the one they decided on entered into her, became her.'

I said, 'You don't think she would have noticed he was getting in?' managing to break out enough coughs to cover my seizure.

'Oh, she may have felt a little dizzy, a little faint for a minute, the way you feel when a bright idea pops into your head from you can't imagine where, becomes a part of you.'

'Now wait a minute, Uncle Nolan!'—all this was going pretty far.

'None of us is the person he started out being but he accepts it without much surprise, in fact may not know when the change began to take place—or that it has taken place. You yourself, Walker,' (with a questioning bead in the telescope eye), 'are possibly not the young man who saw visions?' (No answer.) 'And are possibly not aware of the change?' (No answer.) 'And may not know when you become the old one who dreams dreams.' Then laying me aside for the moment, 'What I'm planning to do,' voice suddenly authoritative, 'is show her round a bit more than I've done, up and down the Highway, show her some of our redeeming qualities, or qualities that may, God willing, redeem us, let her pass them on up. She may not know she's passing them on any more than that camera sending back pictures of the moon but the pictures came through.'

Schurz said, recovered from the shock of it and getting down to brass tacks as best NCO in the Service, 'Maybe we ought to drive her up to Cape Canaveral, Captain, let her shoot some of the way-out stuff up there.'

But Nolan brushed it off. 'No use sending Mr. C pictures of that sort of thing, Schurz, you might as well report on arithmetic problems to the Institute of Advanced Studies——'

'Uncle Nolan,' (I had been as patient with screwy clients in my time)——

'I'd like to send him some pictures of good simple family people—you and your missus, Ashalom, Dudo (I'm not so sure about Dudo)—the life they lead, take her up to The Home Place, Walker, let her meet Iona and Livonia and Stacy, let her go to church with them' (I wanted to say, Go *where?* but naturally didn't); 'some shots of that would probably surprise him after what he's heard, the people all behaving themselves, decent, respectful, all of them with an inkling of understanding, just an inkling, of the Experiment inside each of them buzzing away like a gyro, a stabilizer system, perhaps like the buzz of far-off voices singing *Ein' Feste Burg ist Unser Gott*, anyway reducing the roll—I think he'd be surprised. I'd want her particularly to get a shot of Livonia, the Future you know, and Livonia's young man' (I almost told him I didn't photograph well), 'you said she was getting married, didn't you?'

'No sir, I don't believe so.'

He said he must have dreamed it and I said I didn't see how he had room to dream it, but he just went on that she

certainly would be soon and he would like to send up some
pictures of the wedding—'sweet little girl, I remember her
well, must be a lovely young lady now.' I went along by
saying she had won a beauty contest at college (skipping
the detail that it was Fraternity Row's black-market competition for "Miss Erection of 1969") and came back to the
wedding idea, it seemed to appeal to him. 'The blushing
bride?' I said and he said, 'Quite so. Pictures of decent
upright everyday people it wouldn't be fair to destroy. And
while we're there I'll have Addison bring my will up to date
and get Dr. Arthur to give me that physical Schurz is pester-
ing me about, and give Schurz one too, do you hear that,
Schurz? it'll be like Norfolk, with the freight boat waiting
and all those potatoes,' wrapping it up with a shake of the
head and 'Of course this would have to wait until the messages are all in.'

'You're not looking for any *more*, are you, Uncle Nolan?'

'No, but he may think of something he wants to tell me.'

I broke away from it by saying we might be able to get
some family pictures right there on the Keys if the light
held good, that Stacy might be in Miami on business some-
time soon and might stop in. 'He may bring Livonia,' the
idea flashing in my head of phoning Stacy to bring her,
that Nolan wanted to see her, (as well as the idea of Sisterbaby and me running through some of Mollenbrink's exercises
there in the lascivious Gulf-Stream winds or in the Stream
itself indeed).

'Coming here?' He might have found a Christmas bonus
in his envelope.

I said there was a good chance of it and he said to call
Stacy and make sure. 'All we'd need then, Schurz, would
be to have Helga take the pictures. I'm delighted, Walker,'
turning back to the 'insert' then and asking Schurz if he

would kindly see to putting it in the proper place, Schurz coming in good-naturedly with 'You speak and I jump, Captain.'

(I did phone—twice—but got no answer. They were probably conferring with Sisterbaby, or had been and were just too shaken up to answer.)

4

STACY AND MAMMA jingled in about 10:45 in a rented Bug. I said, 'You didn't bring Sisterbaby? where's Sisterbaby? he wanted you to bring Sisterbaby!' the thought of Sisterbaby at home in the house alone and all the devilment she could think up to get into giving me goosebumps even there in the blinding sun bouncing off the stucco of the *Ship-n-Shore*. 'He wants Sisterbaby.'

Stacy said, 'Come over here, keep your mouth shut, don't bother your mother, she's wild' (Mamma unloading the VW under a grim sort of work-as-therapy cloud, not exactly wild but certainly dangerous). Stacy was wilder, spitting out 'Where's your gin?' and following me over the powdered shells to the *Red Man's*, not saying anything more until we had taken the gins to a table by a back window looking on the Cove and some down-at-heel shrimp boats and then asking me in an accusing tone, 'What's all the stink?' in reference to the various chunks of newly- and not-so-newly captured marine life in a wind-blown shed on a pier. I shrugged it off, and after a minute or two, the gin dribbling down like a TV aspirin and coating things over, he took a deep breath and said, 'She wants to get married, that's what she wanted to tell us, told us last night.'

'Mamma?'

'Wanted to do it tomorrow but we talked her out of a week, we said wait a while for God's sake, at least wait until we can get out from under Christmas. She said NOW! with that throaty laugh of hers, you know the one. I didn't get it at first but your mother got it,' finishing the gin and setting the glass down hard, the bop! seeming to trigger one of his attacks that were like uncorking a bottle of Arkansas champagne.

I said more or less for form's sake, 'Who're you talking about, Stacy?' the words coming out in somebody else's voice because I knew he was going to say just what he did say which was, 'Who? Livonia. Thought at least she might have told you.'

It was such an impossible piece of information when it was actually out in the air, the stink, I couldn't think what to say, impossible on the basis of that chained-to-a-grocery-cart-like-a-dog business and because there had been no indication she had changed her attitude either toward the grocery cart or the dog or me (why change? we had it made) and certainly I hadn't changed round to wanting to be chained to a dog like a grocery cart.

I was chattering to myself in this sort of unreasonable but normal panic resistance when it began to come to me that Stacy wasn't really behaving as if he had the gun on me. I thought of going big-eyed-innocent and asking him who else was getting married tomorrow-week but I was still too afraid, unreasonably or not (it wasn't really practical), of hearing 'You are, son' to chance it and I said nothing, waited while he stared at the back of his hand then turned it over and stared at the front then said with an old-fashioned parental befuddlement, the words appearing to me to have no connection with what we were talking about, 'Leon, it seems.'

I said stupidly, 'What about Leon?' and he snapped at me, 'What do you think I'm doing, Walker, just sitting here enjoying this fish-stink talking to myself? where'd you cut off? she wants to marry Leon.'

'*Mollenbrink!*' It was preposterous.

'She said Mollenbrink.'

After a while I said (it seemed better to keep talking, whatever the words, the way it helps to curse a banged finger), 'What does Mollenbrink say?'

He said they didn't know, hadn't asked. 'If you're unlucky enough to be a parent today you learn not to meddle in the children's marriages,' and I stammered something like What do you know! and Can you tie that! no run-of-the-mill obscenity up to handling it. (I knew exactly what had happened, the bitch figuring that after all I was only a fucking disciple and here was the Master in person right down the road on Zinnia Circle, why not heat up the Great Dick himself? after which, the Livonia-eyes fixing on him like the light in a soldering pistol and Mollenbrink turning to juice.) 'Isn't this all rather sudden?' I said, as don't-care as I could make it, and he said well it seemed she had just found out yesterday morning.

'Found out?'

'Nearly two months along, I believe,' tossing it off in his role of modern-parent-not-nosing-into-none-of-his-business-but-w i s h i n g-at-the-same-time-he-could-keep-baby-o u t-of-a-commune, then going wistful for a second and admitting he couldn't understand it, a girl with every advantage. 'Always had everything she needed, Walker, I mean a car so she could go to college, date in her own back seat—she didn't want the one we bought her but we bought it, and then bought the little scooter she did want—clothes, enough pills to get her through Freshman year,' giving the table two or three patient raps. 'Your mother was pretty upset, fit to be tied in fact, "we'll never live it down" and all that. I told her not to take it so hard, there'd been shotgun weddings ever since the invention of gunpowder, "Used a bow-and-arrow before that," I told her, "Cupid's always got a bow-and-arrow, hasn't he?" trying to cheer her up. But that wasn't what bothered her, the gun bit. It was that Livonia could be so God-damned stupid. People would say she'd neglected her, hadn't raised her right, hadn't explained things. And they probably will.'

He couldn't help tacking on, 'Well, that's the way the ball bounces,' slapping the table again in what was a sort of sigh and saying it was just something we would all have to live with, then adding abruptly as if to show he was on top of it, 'But to get back. The inter vivos, Walker, the thirty Gs, you got him squared away on that of course, was that what you were saying on the phone?' (he knew it wasn't, just an extra push on the needle).

I couldn't say anything for a minute, a little upset as I was. And upset at being upset. I'm a now man, as now as you can be in the provinces with the natural time-lag knocking twelve to fifteen months off the Yankee now. I'm with it, almost; not much with the spike yet, joints of course but the heavy stuff doesn't work out too well in the sticks for the simple reason you need a certain amount of lonesomeness and frustration for it to have something to bite into and with everybody knowing you and your business it's hard to be lonesome long enough to go to the bathroom. Except for that, I think I'm reasonably out (maybe it's *in* now); no trouble about the shithouse language, the houses right there at your elbow for reference like vocabulary builders. And yet it still gets me to find there's another man in the bed too, particularly when it's your sister's bed. And particularly if she's the one pulled him in there, which in this bed I didn't question—the bed idea leading me to blurt out, 'And you left her in town alone? with the freak just down the road!' my answer delivered in a capering sort of triple horn blast through the side window from Sisterbaby shoulder-to-shoulder with Mollenbrink in a bright green rented (or stolen) Continental convertible; maybe it had taken them all this time to find just the right green, more likely I figured they had stopped off on some double bed along the road or in some palmetto bush or both.

I hauled her suitcase out of the car for her (it's better not to let them see they've cut you or they'll cut you again— Mollenbrink in the office, Stacy gone with Mamma), told her I'd only reserved one room, didn't know anybody else was coming. She said, 'What do you mean, Walker love-bee? Leon's getting a room,' and I said, 'I'm talking about you, you can't sleep with Mamma and Stacy, you'll need a bed to sleep in, won't you? for God's sake,' booming the lid of the trunk. She said she was sleeping with Mollenbrink, which annoyed me under the circumstances, hearing it in so many words (annoyed at myself to begin with for not seeing that coming and taking her straight on to his room without ask-ing—the bastard leaving the office for a second and handing me the key as if he took me for the nonexistent bellhop).

Unlocking the door I said as colorlessly as possible that I'd heard it rumored she was getting married and I hoped she would accept my sympathy, hoped they both would. She said they were made for each other, she had an orgasm if he took out even a cigarette and I said, 'Bathroom, bath, shower, basin, hopper' (it seemed impoliter than 'john'), turning on her with, Did she think it was level to pass off one man's child on another man to bring up? (I don't know how I managed to hit on so many brainless things to say but I was griped). She said she wasn't doing that, and I flushed the john as the only answer I could think of.

'It's his, Walker honeybun. Just set it on the bed, love, Leon'll put it somewhere later,' voice drooping and somehow changing the 'it' she was talking about, and I said, 'I know just where he'll put it too,' trying to be as fetid as possible, going on to say, 'I wish you'd tell me beforehand next time you're planning to bring somebody into my bed'—which made no sense at all I admit (it was her bed, usually) except that it gave me a chance to drop the thing nastily on the wall-to-wall and get out talking instead of crawling away like a half-mashed roach.

During the afternoon there were calls back and forth at the ministerial level, Stacy and Iona on Nolan (pointedly not on Mrs. L, with Mamma's 'Don't let us keep you, my dear, you must have *loads* to do'—dishes in the sink, beds, wash on the line), Nolan and Mrs. L (as pointedly included as earlier excused) on Stacy and Iona and Livonia and Mollenbrink ('So pleased!' 'Delighted!' 'Dear Uncle!' 'He's looking so well!'—things were 'looking so well' you could see the silver wires on Stacy's back teeth), Stacy and Mollenbrink on Nolan (evening by then), Schurz and I out on the fringes and Mrs. L humming Schubert snatches over a mixing bowl in the kitchen but called in by Nolan now and then, to catch a few candids with the camera I suppose.

I had a feeling we were getting down to rock now though no mention was made of anybody's dreams or visions or finances or expectations, Stacy not one to let grass grow under his feet with a motel bill for four ticking away, chewing at his credit cards like a goat, the home office at the mercy of Birlant and the girls. It also looked like a bedrock call from the stare Mollenbrink injected into Nolan like an acupuncture needle, twirling it while Stacy held him still with nervous chatter of this and that, referring to Mollenbrink as Mister not to alarm the patient and accounting for his presence with a by-the-way, 'son-in-law, *ex*-son-in-law I should say' (running too much of a temperature to have the details right), the son-of-a-bitch-in-law looking like a Viennese used-car salesman with his chinfuzz and the sideboards we used to laugh at Argentineans for. Nolan rocked hospitably in his wicker rocker indulgently feeding them questions he thought they might enjoy answering, as resourceful in trying to amuse them as a grandmother when the children stopped by from school. He had Mrs. L break out the limeade (big deal! Stacy couldn't believe his eyes) and some sort of *küchen* I hadn't seen before, practically said he hoped their mothers wouldn't mind. He said of course 'we' wanted to do something for them while they were at Pelican, perhaps dinner in the *Red Man's* private room, he would speak to Iona, drifting off under the red-man impetus to tell them about the Mayan ancestors of Florida's Caloosa Indians, which naturally brought the call into the homestretch.

Stacy handled him as delicately as an heirloom watch with the crystal gone, tilted him gently to this topic and that as if to show Mollenbrink-horologist where the hour hand was bent and seemed to hang up on the minute hand, Mollenbrink contributing nothing to the good-fellowship, intent on the patient (Hippocratic Oath and all), on sucking up a syringeful of betrayals from Nolan's unsuspecting veins, and then, as if capping a specimen bottle, bringing the whole visit to a timely end by telling Nolan, apropos of nothing (a stock item with him), of a nurseryman named Hix planting a lawn for a young Mrs. Grady, she busy nearby in white shorts setting out small plants in a border, kneeling, bending, up-ending, until Hix couldn't stand it any longer and leaned

on his rake and said, 'Mrs. Grady, I'd give anything in this
world to get in bed with you.' Mrs. Grady said, 'The charge
is a thousand dollars, Mr. Hix, now get on back to your
grass,' and Hix went off and set in a few roots while he
thought and came back and said, 'What's the down payment,
Mrs. Grady?' (for Hix read Mollenbrink, I suspected, for
Mrs. Grady read Livonia Vidrine, for a thousand dollars
read a bent nickel—and no down payment).—Nolan said
he didn't hold with buying on time and brought up that bit
again about Panurge eating his corn whilst it was still but
grass, Stacy signaling me all the while to come outside, flick-
ing thumb, nodding, rolling eyes toward the VW until a
halfwit would have understood, as if he wanted to finalize
emptying a till (in a way I guess it was that), Mollenbrink
pausing at the kitchen door as they left to study Mrs. L's
bottom as she stirred the mixing bowl, the stirs rippling up
arms, across shoulders, down spine and breaking in a shiver
like wavelets before a puff of wind in the Cove.

We got togther in Stacy's room, Stacy, Mamma, Mollenbrink, Jack Daniel and I (Sisterbaby was in the other room
dressing—or undressing, bitch). I had borrowed one of the
dream quintuplicates from Schurz to put through the meat
grinder (signed for it as if we were still at Angoulême)
and Mollenbrink flipped through it and tossed it on a bed:
'Erotic fantasies,' says he, the fastest drawer of conclusions
in the West, Stacy giving a nod that signified 'Of course,'
as he would have done if a garage man had told him, 'Split
grommet on the distributor bushing.'

I said, 'How could that be, Leon? there's not a woman
in the whole quintuplicate.'

He lifted long-suffering fingers in a request for patience
and started explaining in a pro-to-amateur voice that the
nightmares were caused by (I translate) Nolan's rePressed-

byterian childhood which, following a probably prenatal semi-strangulation, was throwing a lot of raw sewage into his drainage system and polluting his God-given impulse to, as he put it in nursery terms, fuck Mrs. Littleberry. Stacy said, 'God damn it, Leon, there's a lady in the room!' knocked back to Squaresville, of which he was of course the mayor and city manager.

Mollenbrink threw in some sort of on-the-wing vulgarity like, Was there room in the lady? going on, 'Get him into bed with the housekeeper and the nightmares—with the right professional guidance—will correct themselves, a superficial examination of her leads me to the prognosis Mr. Bennett won't have enough juice by morning to know whether he wants his eggs up or over.'

Stacy looked at him and Mamma did too, it had come out so fast, was so packed with contingencies. After a while Stacy said, 'Would he be able to sign his name, Leon, put his X on a deed, an inter vivos?' voice half choked with the wriggling possibilities behind it and Mollenbrink said, 'Maybe, if you helped him hold the pen.'

Mamma said, 'Wait a minute!' in italics and Stacy signaled her to wait a minute herself and said he didn't know, he didn't know, wouldn't it be just handing Mrs. Littleberry a ready-made old-time breach-of-promise suit? if there were such things any more, and Mollenbrink said, Well, it didn't have to be Mrs. Littleberry, 'Somebody else if you prefer, Mrs. Schurz? Mrs. Ship-n-Shore? Iona? Sisterbaby?——'

'I'd prefer you go on the hell back to your patients at home, Leon.' I believe the specter of the bill was beginning to raise its ugly head again because when Mollenbrink said, Ethics! professional ethics! he couldn't abandon a patient at the stage of diagnosis, treatment was what mattered, Stacy said we didn't want to take advantage of his generosity just because he was in the family or as good as, that Leon had to make a living like the rest of us, we understood that. Which Mollenbrink dismissed with an unreliably magnanimous mumble into the chin-bush, 'Let's not worry about that now, the patient is what matters,' something in the words or tone that was delicately unreassuring to a free-loader's ears though it was hard to put your finger on.

We covered a number of other angles before getting anywhere—the need for a confidential stand-by notarized memo from physician-in-charge (Mollenbrink) to next-of-kin (Mamma) summing up his diagnosis as to the soundness (unsoundness) of the patient's mind and memory just in case a sneaky codicil should crawl by us and we had to go to court; we discussed Mrs. L as medication, Mamma very negative with 'it's idiotic to think anybody lucky enough to have a bed of her own would want to bring in somebody else, what's giving him dreams is she's poisoning him, putting drugs in all that sauerkraut and pumpernickel, that's what's giving him dreams,' (Mollenbrink a little annoyed I thought at the reflection on his qualifications as wizard but nothing like annoyed enough to consider washing his hands of the case, suggesting in fact that Walker might well bring 'her' over for a consultation, 'or one thing and another,' giving me a fine-drawn glance as when you watch to see whether your hook is going to the bottom or not); we weighed my idea of loading up and taking Nolan home, if the messages had ended which, with a peaceful last-night, I believed they had (what more did they need to tell him, for Godsake?) though I remembered he had said at one point they seemed to come in like the *New York Times*, none for two or three days (then one then none) then a wheelbarrowload—a likeable idea for Stacy, the motel bill ticking away under him like a timebomb but not practical, they said, not meeting the problem, the problems. 'We don't want him home, Walker, we want him in the bughouse where he belongs,' turning

then to Mollenbrink: 'All right, Leon, what do we do? how
do you put somebody away? For his own good, to keep him
from harming himself and other people.'

Mollenbrink said he wasn't familiar with Florida laws,
if there were such things, they would have to go to Key
West and get a fill-in from somebody at the courthouse,
and Stacy, impatient to get on with it, said, 'Take Nolan,
you mean?'

'Not yet, not yet, see what they want, they might not
need him.'

'Okay, Leon, you've got a car, you've got gas!'

Mollenbrink said two ears were better than one (meaning
four than two of course but his two were already hearing
Sisterbaby's lascivious taps on the wall and his attention was
going to pieces) and Stacy said, All right, he would go along,
they would go in the morning, Mollenbrink giving him the
lifted hand for Silence! and 'Just a minute!' watching the
wall as if he could see girl-skin through it then stumbling
out with his eyes glazed like a concupiscent fish's, Stacy down-
ing his Jack Daniel in annoyance at the interruption and
after a grumpy pause wading again into the sticky bog of
costs. 'This thing could run into money,' (to us, as if we
were shoving it), '*is running* into money,' going on with talk
about the business he was losing at home (Birlant couldn't
remember a phone number long enough to dial it), about
conducting four so-called adults on an all-expenses-paid tour
of Florida junglegyms. '*Five!* My God, I forgot about you,
Walker. He's got us over a barrel.'

I said, 'Mollenbrink?' and he said, 'I'm talking about
Nolan has, what do you mean, Walker? Leon wouldn't be
bastard enough to throw a bill at us after a honeymoon trip
with me picking up the tab' (he couldn't resist 'tab'), 'I
figure a couple of bottles of bourbon on his doorstep if
everything turns out right, after all——'

Mamma said, 'Get rid of her.'

'Rid of who, bun?'

'Get her out of here!'

'Mrs. Littleberry?'

'Whatever her slimy name is.'

'Yes but how——'

'Pay her. Buy her off.'

'You don't know what you're saying, bun. If somebody's got a fair shot at thirty thousand and a long shot at God knows what, three hundred, a million, five million, you can't just "buy her off"—and have anything left for the supermarket.'

An idea for a solution had been entering into me almost as unnoticed as the Agent entering into Mrs. L, an idea as simple as it was elegant, and I broke into the buy-her-off business with 'Do you want an answer to your problem?' It rocked them a little, as I meant it to do, Stacy trying to keep the initiative with 'It's your problem too, son,' which I ignored. I said we wanted to give Uncle a hand-up into the bin, didn't we? all right, all we needed to do (he had said as much himself) was wake him up every time he tried to dream, 'Shake him every time his eyelids start to flicker.'

Stacy almost panicked in the search for a hole in it like somebody slapping his pockets with the law there in the window mumbling, 'See your license.' In a minute he said, 'How you going to get anybody to wake him up? Who? The housekeeper? You? The bedbugs?' I said anybody could wake him up, covering over the fact I hadn't gone into it that far yet—the answer to his question knocking at the door though of course nobody could foresee it was the answer. Stacy said, 'Get it, Walker, it may be a telegram from Birlant,' which I was glad to do, the moans already beginning to seep in from the next room, the honeymoans.

A boy-young-man with hair like a paintbrush dipped in black lacquer was smiling with his head on one side to make room for the cat on his other shoulder (who hit the floor at the sight of me with a thump like a basketball and bounced away): the Captain had sent him for Mr. Walker Bennett.

'Williams,' I said, 'Walker Williams.'

He said, 'No sir, the Captain said Bennett,' and I said, 'I can't help what the Captain said, he meant Bennett—Williams, I mean,' and we argued about it for a minute until I asked him to just take me instead and he said he would, 'Soon as I find Delia,' whistling for her in four or five notes in a minor key.

On the sea-going bridges mooring Pelican to ugly reality (he gave up on Delia but said it didn't matter, she knew her way) he said everybody called him Jack but his name was Chak, after his 4-greats-grandfather Chakika, 'Caloosa chief, hanged for all to see near Lake Okeechobee by Lieutenant Colonel William S. Harney in 1840'—as well as I could understand him round a white helmet with 'Chak VII' painted on it in red and over the jackhammer cylinders of the Suzuki 750 and through the next-room moans that followed me like banshees, though I managed at last to switch over to Mollenbrink's bill and on to the pleasant hints I'd been picking up here and there that the sex manual wasn't the gold mine it had been, so much competition and the new books with color photographs that even in b/w would have landed him in the jug back in the dark days when his book had appeared (he had tried to get it updated but the publisher was switching to cookbooks as a better investment —'After all, Doctor,' he is supposed to have told Mollenbrink, 'people get hungry three times a day every day'); anyhow I thought it wasn't a question of bill or no bill but of what the bill would look like, Chak gabbling on as if he hadn't been given much of the floor at the pow, about the 750, about the boat (the *Samuel A. Mudd*—I'm not sure I mentioned the name—him screaming something like, 'That's not a shrimp boat, too small,' and me yelling, 'Maybe for small shrimp?'—couldn't help it, once a joke always a joke—and him shrieking, 'Likes her to be a shrimp boat because he likes shrimp, Captain sees it like it suits him,' and me yelping, 'Even so' with the spit blowing out of my mouth), about working round the place at any odd job came to hand, sounding as useful as Other and Miscellaneous on an expense account, all the time the idea grubbing toward the front of my mind, sprouting at last with the sounding-out question of Did he think the Captain was a little beany? and him saying (I think) that his people had a great respect 'for someone granted power to see beyond the tepee'—an amusing boy, as Nolan had said of Ozias, the thought coming with a tied-in sub-thought that Chak was a more likely candidate for Agent than Mrs. L (granting an Agent), and the sub-sub-thought—revelation, rather—that Chak was the one to shake him, one for odd jobs round the place. All the family had to do was pick out the bin. And make a reservation, there'd be a line.

I said, (we were slowing down for the turnoff at Nolan's mailbox and the words came out as if a gag had been pulled out of my mouth), 'You may not know it, Chak, but the Captain's been having bad dreams——'

'The reason I went to the pow,' he said, 'to talk to Grandpa, he's our medic, told him all about them—Grandpa Chakika, the Fifth, I'm Seventh. He killed a chicken, fed the liver to the alligator, then the head, went through the whole show A to Z; he says nothing to worry about, Captain's getting ready to up anchor, everything aboard, all stowed away tight and tidy, just waiting for the wind to come round——'

I said, Yes, well, er, ahem, cough-cough, it seemed to us in the meantime the nightmares were endangering his health and as closest of kin we couldn't allow that; 'We want somebody in the room with him to help him if he gets another one—maybe there won't be any more, we hope not, what else have they got to tell him?—but if one should start after him, somebody in the room to wake him up.'

We were on the ground and he was rolling the 750 into the tool shed; he stopped as he was getting an old towel off a nail: 'Break his dream?'

It didn't sound very cooperative and I maneuvered a little by saying I supposed Mrs. Littleberry could do it, right there anyhow, just kick him, but she needed her sleep, and he said Miss Helga slept down the hall. 'Doesn't sleep with the Captain?' 'Sleep with—Oh Mr. Bennett!' and we were off the subject.

I said, Never mind, and left him—on his knees giving Suzuki a going over as if she had run the Derby; I felt I had done the ground work though, poured the footings.

5

OF COURSE MANY details of the disaster only came to me later but I think it makes more sense if I run them in where they belong, what sense there is to be made. Many of them, now that I look back, must have been planned, whipped into shape, in beds of one description or another in which I naturally wasn't present: I don't doubt that Mrs. L's exit or incarceration was discussed in Stacy's and Mamma's bed (or beds—vide supra), and I am quite certain that the Vidrine-Mollenbrink-Williams-(Bennett) exit from Pelican was discussed with Mrs. L in Nolan's (or *from* Nolan's— I don't really get the picture of whether Mrs. L was seated or flat), and it is more than likely that Mr. and Mrs. *Ship-n-Shore* continued to kick us around when they went to bed or beds, and it is possible, if not so likely, that Nolan's exit, the putting-away-for-his-own-good one, was discussed by the son-of-a-bitch and the bitch herself in the motel bed of Room 18 which in spite of myself I shared in about the same nightmarish way Nolan shared for a time Mr. C's hypothetical office. I mean, if you get right down to the grass roots they look very much like the coils in an innerspring mattress.

As I put it together, back together, at just about the minute Mamma was raising her voice at Stacy to 'Get rid of her' (as if he could), Nolan was saying to 'her,' 'I'm wondering if *Donald* can't think of some way to get rid of these people maybe, or Ashalom, pack them off I don't care how, they bother me I don't know exactly why, something about them' (Donald Dudo, franchisee-in-law of the *Ship-n-Shore* by marriage to Mrs. Maple's widowed sister who held the franchise), 'do they bother you? I think they bother Delia.'

'Bother me?' noncommittal, always noncommittal.

'I'd really rather you had nothing to do with them, I——'

'But certainly.'

'I have a feeling something has gone wrong with their sense of beauty—dear me!'

'Yes? What is it?'

'I overlooked telling Schurz about when Mr. C said to me, "A sign something has gone wrong with the Experiment,

Nolan, is if something goes wrong with the sense of poetry," dear me.'

'I'll tell him, I'll see he puts it in,' giving the old apple a little higher polish. 'Thank you, my dear, thank you. Now I think I'll call Donald, see what he can do, ask him to come over, he'll be glad to help.' 'I'll call him for you.' 'I don't like to trouble you, Helga my dear.' 'No trouble.' 'You're too good to me.' 'My pleasure.' And on into the dovecot routine that I wouldn't inflict on anybody if I knew the exact words which I'm glad to say I don't.

I'm not sure whether they invited Dudo or not or even tried to call him, it's all a little indistinct and cryptic in here like crab-shapes under the bridges when you can't be certain you see crabs or water-shadows, can't be certain of anything except that whatever it is is not where you think it is. Or when. The day seems like Sunday but it must have been at least Monday because the County Judge wouldn't have been in her office on Sunday (chambers), or Ashalom's aunt at her nearby Underwood who told him at dinner of two men talking to the Judge about declaring somebody incompetent who lived on Pelican Ashalom would know who it was but she didn't catch the name—which brought about Ashalom's stopping off (on his way up) to ask after the Captain's health, being reassured by Mrs. L (Nolan was taking a cold shower), after which he retraced a few bridges and made a slow demoralizing circuit of the tags parked round the swimming pool of the *Ship-n-Shore*, saluted Dudo big-eyed by the ice machine, tilted his mirror a fraction on account of the Key West sun and gunned away for Miami.

If they invited Dudo the chances are he was picking up the phone to invite himself anyway, about to burst his con- stipated gut all swollen with the guesses and assumptions and babble-babble he had been accumulating through his miscellaneous snoopings (and Mrs. Dudo's), all worthless until he could lay them against the proper ear, Nolan's, and even more immediately uncomfortable under the suggestiveness of Ashalom's prowl-past, the sort of thing to start anybody thumbing through the shady deals he's been up to within the Statute of Limitations. I could see them from the bathroom where I was running a comb through the walnut-brown moustache that was giving Mrs. L nightmares of her very own though she wasn't telling, Nolan shaking Dudo's hand hot off the gold wheel of *his* Cadillac, Schurz rolling in like a volunteer fireman (Nolan had no doubt sent for him).

By the time I reached the kitchen and had them lined up between the new café curtains Mrs. L had strung in the windows—Mrs. L moving about behind me perfumed in veal scallops with port wine—they were in chairs on the stern of the *Samuel A. Mudd* (for privacy) bent over toward each other like a three-sided parenthesis as if their voices could have carried across the yard from the dock, Schurz with the clipboard (just in case), and Dudo in his Royal Poinciana shirt smoking cigarettes and flipping them over the side and spilling everything he had gathered up about us through walls, round corners, under beds, in trash baskets, out of garbage cans like a bald-headed scavenger cat—all his tittle-tattle of course on a direct wire to Mrs. Maple's extended ears and the great beyond (not that what he was saying amounted to a row of bent pins except for its effect on Nolan, who sat through most of it without much comment beyond an occasional 'I don't believe it!' or 'can't' or 'You must be mistaken!' with different thicknesses of underlining for the 'must,' all of it interspersed with a random mumbled 'I knew it!' in various keys).

It began by Nolan's saying—old relic of the cash-and-carry economy—he couldn't have Dudo lose money by putting 'these people' out, he would rent the three rooms himself, 'Say, for a week, Donald, beginning at check-out time tomorrow if that's agreeable.' Donald would only need to tell them the space was reserved from tomorrow on, very sorry. 'If they ask to be shifted to other rooms, Donald, you're booked solid; if necessary I'll engage your whole inn.'

Dudo was too freshly out of pinchgut New England to be able to pretend this wouldn't be satisfactory, but also too old-Plymouth-Rock to have Nolan figuring on more rooms than would do the job and he said, 'It's just two rooms, Captain,' in a not-that-it-mattered tone while he thought a minute.

Nolan said, 'All right, Donald, I'll engage those two— *two* rooms?' practically adding it all up on his fingers.

'Just two, yes sir.'

'Oh, the ladies in one, the gentlemen in the other,' Nolan explained to himself, tossing in a parenthesis that Stacy was tight, and Dudo said, 'No sir, Mr. and Mrs. in 17, Mr. What's-his-name and the young lady in 18.'

It threw Nolan into a ridiculous old-time hard-rubber-tire skid, but he pulled out of it with a ready, 'Secretly married, Donald?'

'They say they're getting married next week. Or she does.'

Nolan said next week was next week but this was this week and Dudo started giving instances of the hotel business as a liberal education and Nolan brought him back in the road by saying there was something down-at-heel about premarital cohabitation (you hear everything if you keep listening) and he didn't hold with it. 'The parents? What do the parents say?'

Dudo said they seemed pleased—except that the mother acknowledged to his wife she hadn't been too pleased when she first learned the young lady was expecting, it seemed so stupid and the young lady wasn't really stupid. Nolan said, 'What is the young lady expecting, Donald?' as if it might be a parcel-post package or last week's *Times*, though of course he was only trying to snatch a second or two of grace to decide where to store the answer in his attic-dried bag of quaint provincialities. Dudo glanced off to sea through his upper lenses and settled it on Nolan's terms with 'A blessed event, it seems, Captain' and Nolan used one of his futile you-must-be-mistakens, pressing on the must.

'No sir, Mrs. Vidrine told my wife, said of course they would have felt better to have the young lady marrying the father but that wasn't feasible, and nowadays with inflation and students and all did it matter——'

'The young lady is in a family way but not by the man she is marrying?'

'To the best of my understanding, yes sir. Her brother, I understand.'

'What about her brother?'

'He's the father, I understand, probably the father, there seems to be some question——' not finishing for Nolan's slapping both palms on the starboard rail and standing up until his scalp was against the awning and mumbling at the misty edge of the sea, 'Every imagination of the thoughts of their hearts is only evil continually.'

'There are some other little things, Captain.'

Nolan asked him if he would be so kind as not to tell him any more right then but Dudo was going downhill and couldn't stop, crack-of-the-door tattletales that ranged all the way from 'a deed on some property' they wanted Nolan to sign and help him get out from under his Lifetime Exemption (or get his LE off his back in cash as a $30,000 wedding present, he would naturally want to 'do something' for the bride—'Not a bad little pinch of snuff, Schurz, would you say?') to such everyday things as incense sticks burning in the rooms to cover the joints (what's a better way?), ending with a story of the ladies telling his wife the Captain was dissatisfied with Mrs. Littleberry. 'Dissatisfied with Mrs.

Littleberry?' Yes sir, and asking his wife if she would help them find a new (and operationally married) housekeeper, planning at Mrs. Littleberry's departure to move in with him, one or the other of them, and run the house for him, not to put him to any inconvenience——

'Get them out, Donald!'

'Mr. Mollenbrink seems to be an author.'

'Whatever it takes. I can't go into all of it now, how important it is, some day I will, but *get rid of them!*'

Dudo said he wished Nolan could see a copy of the author's book, which had to be seen to be believed—I think he was already sidestepping any promise to 'get rid of them,' though Nolan didn't seem to notice, turning to Schurz with, 'They're just the sort of people he was talking about, Schurz,' which Schurz didn't seem ready to deny. 'Thrown out the Experiment like an old bicycle tire, or never knew it was in them.'

Dudo said as they were 'doing' 18, he and Mrs., the book fell open to a photograph and his wife screamed like a crab had her, but Nolan ignored it, if he heard it at all, sitting down again hands on his kneecaps watching a black-headed gull on the tube of the telescope or looking in that direction, maybe he was looking for a smoke signal from Dr. Mudd. He said, 'If she finds out, Schurz,' and stopped for so long Schurz came in helpfully with 'Yes sir' at which Nolan went on, 'There's nothing she can do but shoot it, we can't ask her not to.—You *must* be mistaken, Donald.'

Donald said cannibalism was the only thing he'd want to say he hadn't come on evidence of 'so far' and Nolan made a large gesture toward Miami and said, 'Get rid of them, Donald, what's your check-out time? maybe they can go today.'

Any well-brought-up Southerner—even if I sound like Nolan—would have left it at that, gone back to the motel

and later told Nolan there was going to be a little delay
but he would go on trying, the soft demur; Dudo had to
give it the old rockbound-coast treatment, standing at the
top of the gangplank with his chin out and saying, No, he
wouldn't do it, he wouldn't put guests out on the highway
without cause.

'Without cause!' says Nolan.

'If they took it up with Kansas City I'd be in all kinds of
soup.'

Nolan was so unacclimated to the down-East negative he
didn't know how to answer. He asked Dudo if he meant
to say they could stay as long as they liked and Dudo said
if they had enough credit cards it did, they hadn't created
any trouble, hadn't disturbed other guests, nobody had com-
plained, and Nolan fell back into an antiquated Stars-and-
Bars politeness that left him almost disagreeing with himself.
I suppose he was also thinking it was still not the occasion
(Dudo at the gangplank) to go into who Mrs. L really was,
explain to him her status as Agent and the towering reason
it was so important—*so important?*—to get rid of these
people, not easy to explain in the first place even with plenty
of time.

In any case he walked over to Dudo with a faint Southern
smile and, to end on a note of concord by finding something
Dudo could agree to, asked if Dudo would phone him as
soon as he knew when 'the party' would be going, at which
Dudo nodded, stumbled off big-footed down the cleats and
cranked up the Cadillac with a chord like the Bostons starting
on Brahm's C-major, Nolan and Schurz regarding each
other across the width of the deck, motionless and silent in
the midst of the restless squeaking water birds and now and
then the long zoom of a plane going over hijacked to
Havana (it was those days) or the short one of a truck on
the bridges, sunup or sundown you couldn't tell which.

Schurz said he was disappointed in Donald, giving the top of his ball-point a few sympathetic taps on the clipboard as Nolan was reminding him that Balzac 'has it somewhere that innkeepers combine the instinct of a policeman, the astuteness of a spy and the cunning of a shopkeeper,' after which he led the way down the plank, across the yard and into the kitchen as I was sliding my friendly hand between Mrs. L's velvet-coated and apparently astonished thighs.

I don't know when the craving began to take hold, perhaps as far back as the day I came and her skipping in and out of the house with 'sugar for the Sergeant' and all that though I wasn't aware of it then, in no condition to be, as I've explained. Since then Sisterbaby's unspeakable double cross had fertilized the idea, given it some peat moss to grow in, blossom in, and I also wanted to do my part in saving Nolan by getting Mrs. L out of the picture, saving us all indeed. And also of course that day, afternoon, there was the aroma of the scallops in port wine, to say nothing of the stirrings she gave the skillet from time to time which I had noticed Mollenbrink absorbing himself in earlier. Anyway, whatever brought it on, it seemed to take on epidemic proportions while I stood at the window thinking of it and I abandoned the three in the *Samuel A. Mudd* and sat down sideways at the table.

I tend to hang up over openings—the Pawn-to-King-4 bit that means You're off, for better or worse! You're airborne, God help you!—and I fiddled a while with the TV and Freddy Forecast who was trying to see something disastrous enough to be media-worthy in 'a tropical disturbance' way off somewhere tooling along in the direction of South Texas not bothering anybody. It took me back to the other one and I said, cutting him off, 'How did you like Gilda, "Helga my dear"?' putting the familiarity in playful quotes not to scare her, it had always been 'Mrs. Littleberry' before.

She said she didn't know any Gilda, rapping the wooden spoon, (rather edgy I thought, usually a good sign) and I said, 'The little puff you had a week or so back, we name them after girls, makes them more companionable.' She didn't answer except for a couple of swirls at the skillet with the spoon, ignoring the silence which began rising up from the linoleum in chilly ripples.

When it had got so deep it felt like blood-pressure rubbers on both arms I switched over to personalities, sure-fire as a general thing. I said there was something I had been wanting to ask her, taking a good draught from the bottle of port the only thing in reach and trying to think of something (besides who the hell did she think she was, barging in on the rightful heirs like this? and just a little afraid, way down, she would say she was a Factory Representative, a ball I wouldn't know how to, as Stacy would say, pick up and run with).

She turned it off by saying maybe I'd like to make myself useful by setting the table, which somehow seemed to loosen my words and I said that watching her unsettled me so bad I couldn't set a wristwatch, personal enough I should have guessed though it didn't seem to be because she said in that case perhaps I'd like to run out there and see if Mr. Dudo and the Sergeant were staying to supper, if they were it was going to be short helpings.

I paid no attention to such semi-hysteria and it ended with both of us at the cupboard putting on a little do as to who was going to set the table, 'I'll do it,' 'Please!' 'Let me,' hands brushing, arms bumping, hips grazing, and I told her in a suitably offcolor mumble that the Doctor carried a few servings of grass in his medicine bag, looking at her and getting no response and going on that he had asked me to bring her over, maybe tonight, why not? and the four of us would kick it round the floor and see who ended up where—I hadn't cleared it with Mollenbrink but these psychologists can be taken to the cleaners like the rest of us and all that chat about getting Mrs. L into Nolan's bed hadn't fooled me as to whose bed his libidinous unconscious was pulling down the spread of.

She pretended not to understand. 'Kick the grass around?'

'Or speed,' I said, 'he's got speed too if you're worn out on grass. A little, you know? fuck-in, just us four, or six maybe if Mamma and Stacy want in,' all of which would have been no doubt enticing enough if she hadn't been down there for bigger stakes, rights of survivorship and all that, I mean, I'm not talking about espionage, I haven't lost my mind or hadn't at that point.

Even so I could tell she was thinking it over, putting two or three plates shakily on the table, turning them this way and that to kill time and give her tongue a chance to stop drying out so she could say something; another minute would have been enough but of course nothing would do but the phone had to ring like getting a flat halfway up the mountain and I laid my head down on the tablecloth, didn't even watch her flutter out of the door.

'Oh yes, miss!' from down the hall, trying to disguise her heavy breathing (Sisterbaby, obviously—bedside phone snuggled against her bitch-muzzle). 'No, not in at the moment, very sorry . . . (space, space). Yes . . . (space). I will tell him, certainly, oh yes, but . . . (space, space). Tomorrow? I am afraid the Captain will be very busy tomorrow . . . (space, space, space).'—I cut it off with a drag at the port.

I planned to ask her, Busy doing what, for crying out loud? but she came in saying, 'Your sister wants the Captain to go with them to Key West in the morning. "Such a pretty drive," she says. "We see so little of dear Uncle."'

It took my speech for a second or two, Stacy's hand clearly behind it, and the rest of them behind it also (work-

ing themselves up at my way of handling—*not* handling,
to them—'Dear Uncle'); anyway something was afoot,
whether a Key West lawyer's office and an outright grab
at a Deed of Gift covering the LE or, it suddenly popped
in to me, something more drastic such as a date with the
Court, a Judicial Hearing on Dear Uncle's competence? the
ground already prepared, if you believed Ashalom's aunt
which I certainly did—the sum of it all drawing me into a
sort of sexual bog-down that called for a wrecker. I said,
'Forget it, let them worry about it, as I was saying,' trying
to remember what I *was* saying, having trouble reassembling
a few pieces of shattered venery but able in a minute to
come up with 'You loose butterflies in the old jewel bag,
Helga my dear.'

She said, 'Butterflies?' (the shopworn put-off of the back-
quote when you feel things slipping) and I said, 'Come
off of it!' and kissed an ear, the nearest thing, the others
stumbling in the door and still so aghast at Dudo's negative—
to say nothing of the low slander he had shocked them with
—they didn't see she had pushed me into a chair (I felt as
if I had kissed an electric eel) and my hand had got away
from me and begun creeping up like a pickpocket.

But one interruption bowling in mercilessly on top of
another and privacy dispelled for good and all I was as
deflated as I had been once when the night nurse in my
hospital ward defended herself by flipping me hard with
her middle finger (as shoddy a trick as they come) and I
gave up on the whole thing and ate a few disagreeable bites
of the veal scallops in port, Nolan in what I see now was his
own confrontation with the problem he had wished to put
on Dudo, I mean the poser of how to get rid of a guest
without falling back on muscle, an almost cruel predicament
for a Southerner of Nolan's day, queasy at 'scenes,' crippled
by arthritic courtesy, and hamstrung by the simple inherited

fear the guest might refuse to leave and there you would be, 'occupied' again as you had been on a larger scale in 1867-77 which you had heard about from your own, in Nolan's case, father. So Nolan silent—all of us silent—and I not knowing then Dudo had betrayed us, I asked to borrow the car 'to run over to the motel to say goodnight to Mamma' (it sounded even better than I expected); mostly I just wanted to get out of the silences though I also wanted to find out something about this Key West business—and also, not least, where that move left my inspiration about starving him binwards of dreams. Nolan nodded, evidently pleased to get me out of the house even on such a short-term basis.

I thought the trip would take a good deal longer than it did. I could hardly have been gone an hour—maybe fifteen minutes each way, maybe fifteen on each elbow at the *Red Man's*, a matter of seconds in the *Ship-n-Shore* itself: no answer to knocks at 17 ('Gone to the early show,' from Mother Dudo's TV-lounger somewhere up the hall), and to knocks that shook the DO NOT DISTURB on 18 Mollenbrink shouted, 'Go away, can't you read!' I said, 'It's Walker, Leon, I want to talk to you. About tomorrow.' He said he couldn't talk now, could hardly breathe, and I rattled the doorknob and shouted, 'In! Let me in!' and he shouted back, 'Go away! You wouldn't like it here if I let you in,' which tripped a female yelp of everyday bitching merriment. I gave the door a futile but full-bloodied kick from the hip and went to the *Red Man's*.

When I got back Schurz's portable was tapping in Nolan's closed-off bedroom. Nolan's voice came through the taps but I couldn't make out the sense, which the portable seemed to grab out of the air before it reached the door. The only thing you could see through the keyhole was a table and Nolan's self-centered hourglass trickling away (always giving me the feeling, with the telescope, he had posted sentries on the

strategic overlooks. I took it he had had a little snooze
after the scallops and run into God knows what, or who—
a mistake as it turned out but reasonable enough I think,
given the circumstances.

6

THE MORNING BEGAN with Nolan's voice on the phone
coming in through the thin-skinned walls to my pillow
as if floating on the new-day smell of Mrs. L's frying bacon
or on the horizontal beams of the big sun sitting on the Gulf
Stream like a traffic light. '. . . I need him, Mrs. Schurz,
please, soon as he gets up' (Schurz must have been on the
john, reveille long past). 'I'm making notes, tell him, but
it's getting foggier every minute,' as if hanging on to a
slippery porpoise by his fingernails. '. . . yes ma'am, oh, dis-
turbing is no word for it but I didn't like to call him before
sunup . . .'

He didn't seem to mind my joining them (if he saw me
at all—minded the early cigarette smoke maybe), Schurz
with the clipboard, an extra pair of glasses in his shirt pocket
and two spare ball points in case he had a flat, Nolan seeming
to pipe it all down through a searching-out stare up into
the palm leaves lighted on the underside. As well as I
could fill in the few minutes I had missed, Nolan had been
going down the rather worn sapphire steps of the Head-

quarters Building to a sky-taxi waiting at the pearly curb with the motor running or whatever sort of power plant it carried (not the first time he was there I take it, must have gone back another night to straighten out something) when a confident fast-talking somewhat scratchy voice (male), close by but apparently bodiless though Nolan kept searching, asked if Nolan could spare a quarter, adding as Nolan was reaching tolerantly into a pants pocket, 'Quarter of an *hour*, Mr. Bennett.'

Nolan said that was a different matter altogether, the taxi was double-parked and he didn't have any loose time on him anyway, taking a step or two down, trying to break it off, and the Voice mumbled at his ear (still at his ear, as if floating down with him like a TV reporter), 'Yours be the advantage all, Nolan, mine the revenge,' which stopped Nolan cold, naturally.

They sat in a patch of shade from a large fig tree at one end of the steps—at least Nolan did—and the Voice loosed a pent-up tirade against Mr. C which offended Nolan. 'Hold on there!' Nolan said. 'He's been very accommodating to me in all sorts of ways, I don't have to——'

> '*Just a minute, Nolan, I've got some big stuff here. But let me first say why I stopped you, a simple matter of mutual assistance. You need help, I know you're smart enough to see that, and I need help (which I'll explain to you, cards on the table), and as they used to teach us back in First-aeon Algebra, two things needing the same thing need each other.*'
>
> *Nolan said good-naturedly he hadn't taken that course (the air on one side of him seemed to have warmed up more than on the other) and the Voice said, 'Frankly, Nolan, everything is not perfect for me down there, surprising as it may be to you believing things are per-*

*fectly stinking. You're not even perfect fools. You'll
bat it all to hell some day, I'm not worried about that,
but you're taking too fucking long about it. Some of
my people, not many, you understand, a vociferous few—
but before we get into that I want to say I'm interested
in you, Nolan, and in your family too, attractive
folks——'*

Nolan said, 'ATTRACTIVE!' [the small caps in it
rather hurting my feelings as a member of the most
idealistic, most intelligent, best educated Straight-A gen-
erations in history]. *The Voice was good enough to say
our depravity had a charming amateurish quality 'often
useful for drawing in timid souls not yet up to wading
into it whole-hogs—I see I'm going too fast for you,
Nolan, let me pull up and straighten out a few things,'
switching back to talk about 'old C, not ancient but
old-old,' long past retirement age but too full of himself to step down, reactions clumsy, in the way, ideas
antiquated, methods superseded, 'the whole caboodle
superseded. This bird-brain scheme he keeps harping on,
trying to make one animal different from all the rest!
What's the idea? "Sparrows! Fowls of the air! I love
every one of you fellows!" and all the time buttering
up old John Q. Flatfoot. If I was a "fowl of the air"
I'd let loose on his royal bald head, may do it myself
one day if I'm flying by——'*

'Please!'

'*Well, Nolan, is he running a democracy or isn't he?
Does he want equality or doesn't he? Don't ask him
because he couldn't tell you. And wouldn't if he could.*'

'*He told me the other day he couldn't explain it all
to us until our brain had grown a few more convolu-
tions——*'

'*Oh, he's got a warehouseful of handy answers. A thousand varieties of his favorite None-of-your-business.*'

'*He said he had tried to explain it to us in human terms, giving it a family parallel—father-son, reward-punishment, do-this-don't-do-that—but we can't even understand family any more. He said if he made it simple we wouldn't swallow it and if he gave it to us straight we couldn't.*'

'*Throwing his weight around, Nolan! Fitting you out with special left-hand threads so you can't even get a screw (excuse it, Nolan) except through him, or making you think you can't, making you think you can't get along without him when the truth is—hear this, Nolan—* he can't get along without you. *That's what bugs him. He's scared you'll pick up and leave him, as you would if you didn't have to carry all this special equipment that keeps getting out of fix and nobody's allowed to service but him or you've broken the warranty, this useless closed-circuit halfassed transistor in you—useless except to play him back to himself so he'll think he's still in business—you don't like it, naturally you don't it gets in your way, makes you feel inferior.*'

'*The Experiment, you mean?*'

'*It isolates you, Nolan, shuts you off in a corner all by yourself like a battery chicken. He's trying to exile you from the animal kingdom, no reason, just to see what happens. Even now the regular animals don't like you, bristle up when you come round, spit at you, bite you, walk out on you* (run *I should say and as fast as they can go, or hop or fly or crawl), most of them except a few hypocritical dogs. Oh he's impossible!—Wait a minute, Nolan, I'll get you another taxi, let him go.— The point is you want to grow up, be free, get yourself out of solitary which is driving you crazy but you don't know how.'*

Nolan told him he didn't know enough to know what was best for himself and the Voice said, 'That's just it! He's slapped you down there and dumped all these cockeyed puzzles on you and hasn't given you brains enough to know a solution if you step on one, it's like pushing you out on the ice with one skate, no wonder you're always falling on your ass. I know what you want, you want to be free.'

'I don't know, not altogether, not free of everything. There's such a thing as being too free. I suppose you know Ibn Tufail?'

'I know everybody, Nolan, wish I didn't.'

'He said if you free yourself from tradition you will lose all inner security, you will be cast hither and thither and probably come to an evil end.'

'Oh those Orientals! They delight old C like a basket of kittens.'

'It wasn't an Oriental said without tradition mere anarchy is loosed upon the world.'

'The Irish are just as bad.—I'm not talking about tradition, Nolan, I'm talking about growing up. It's not your fault you don't know enough about the way things operate to solve the puzzles, nobody's blaming you, that's the plan, makes you keep running to him, makes him feel important, Big Dog With the Brass Collar. Of course you want to be free. And the only way you can ever be free is to shed this sickly human Difference he likes to talk about, this goosed-up "Experiment." Do you want to be a guinea pig all your life, Nolan? A two-legged hamster? Spirit! He's trying to turn you into a spook, my friend, don't you see that? Spit it out like a milk tooth, you're a big boy now, stand

*up straight, blow your nose. You've come a long way,
Nolan, I say that in fairness to you, over the dead
bodies of one big-shot Dictator after another trying to
hold you down, Ra, Shamash, Helios, I forget all their
funny names, Zeus and that free-wheeling commune on
Olympus, Jehovah and that Troika up in the sky, but
you still can't quite work up your nerve to cut loose,
with your* Something Somewhere—*not on the job every
day, reliable, somebody you could count on like the
Whip, what's his name? Hyperion and his horses (that
was a picture, Nolan! sorry you missed it, worth seeing),
or any old time there was a sassy human cunt around
like Zeus——'*

'*If you please!*'

'*—or once in an age when he happened to remember
you like Jehovah, but what you call* Something, *you
can't even name it, even think it. You've inflated yourselves with gods for so long you're only now getting
smart enough to know you're just a worm, haven't
got a leg to stand on (if you'll excuse the fun, I can't
help it, Nolan, the whole thing is side-splitting if you
back off a few thousand miles—the way you run down
your currency to run up your wages and profits and
create happiness out of thin air), only now catching on
that being affable gets you nothing, it's the horse's
ass who scares the piss out of everybody and brings
home the bacon. . . .'*

(Nolan giving all this in a factual voice as if enumerating
objects on a table, no question they were there, just pointing
them out. And yet there were little drops of sweat on his
forehead that looked different from everyday September-on-
the-Keys sweat, one hand or the other wiping his face now
and then with a morning-creased handkerchief, words coming

through it or round it not to interrupt the dialogue or mono-
logue or whatever you want to call it, at the same time wiping
his good eye which often watered anyhow. It seemed to me
he was giving old Big Mouth the right treatment, letting
him talk—you always hang yourself if you keep talking—
but Nolan was obviously uneasy.)

'. . . . *You're cutting your own throat, Nolan, you
people, and the knife, the rusty razorblade, is pity.
That's where you step outside of the System and your
troubles begin. There's no room for pity, Nolan, it's the
sand in the gearbox or whatever you call the thing, the
monkeywrench in the crankcase. Pity busts it all open.
How are the fittest going to survive with you all spending billions every year fighting for the survival of the
unfit? You all know it but the truth is you haven't got
the guts to face it.—"Can't live by bread alone," remember that old chestnut, Nolan?'*

'*I remember.*'

'*Now I ask you! That's just what you're about to
learn to do—if you listen to me. And don't let your
feet get cold. That sort of talk is like saying you can't
fly without feathers. You've reached a stage of develop-
ment, Nolan, where you're all but free, all but able to
live and breathe in a vacuum, in a great Without.
You're without guilt (but for an ailing few), without
shame, sin, love, without the need to pray, practically
free of grief, of hope (those two used to give you people
fits), you're all but free of illness, all but free of gravity.
All but free of values, Nolan, that's the big one. Cut
that and you're in orbit! What are you scared of? A
little beef, a little booze, a little screw, a little snooze—
godamighty, man, what do you think this is? . . .'*

Nolan's back was to the bridges and Schurz was squiggling shorthand like a hungry chicken and Sisterbaby rolling down the slope in the green Lincoln unseen except by me, and maybe the cat, was like a supplementary nightmare of my very own. I bounced up, pushing at her with taps of my hand as I kicked gray Keys-sand into my shoes hurrying across the yard (they didn't know I had left, if they knew I had been there). The point was clear enough: *they* had sent her to pick him up figuring, knowing, a female finger could twist him round it in half the time it would take any other kind.

'Busy!' I said. 'He's busy, can't see anybody now,' which I had to repeat when she found the automatic connection for lowering the air-conditioned window. 'He's in conference.'

She said, 'What do you mean, Walker? he's right there in front of my nose,' and I said he had a salesman with him from outer space and she started opening the door as if she thought I was kidding. 'I mean it,' I said and stood against the door so it wouldn't open.

'Let me out, love,' with a female sting.

'Didn't you see that DO NOT DISTURB on the mailbox?' (stupid, but it was in the front of my mind, imbedded you might say, and she never fails to bring some kind of stupidity out of me anyhow).

She didn't get the tie-in, went on that 'Daddy' (to distinguish him from Papa long over the dam) was taking him to Key West this morning, all of them were going she had phoned last night hadn't What's-her-name told him? I said, 'No Daddy's not either,' not trying to protect Nolan from them just not able to wipe out the sound-track coming through the other DO NOT DISTURB and meaning to be as unaccommodating as I could, and annoyed too at this high-handed way of bypassing my better solution by taking him straight on to the Judge; that seemed obviously what they were up to, figuring he was ready for the bin now (I wouldn't want to say he wasn't but my plan would have finalized it and anyway you don't care to be bypassed like that).

'Everybody's going,' she said, 'except you and What's-her-name,' giving me the soldering-pistol eye then going on about 'empty house, empty beds,' as if it were a hunk of white meat on a crabbing line—which it certainly was but I was damned if I would grab it, Mrs. L with bigger ideas anyhow. I said, 'Give me a tinkle tonight, I'll see if I can firm it up for tomorrow.'

She said, 'Not tomorrow, *today*,' and I said, 'Or day after tomorrow,' and she said, pushing at the door, 'I want to talk to him,' and I said, 'No chance,' surprised I had it in me.

She persisted with, 'We need to talk to him, Walker,' voice going up. 'We're not getting anywhere with the you-know-what, we don't know what you're up to,' and I said, 'Another day, sugar lump,'—eye to eye and I thought she blinked, even with the door half open and though she went on for a minute or two about 'coming all this way to see him, spending all this money,' about 'Daddy' going up the wall if Nolan didn't.

I said, 'Next week maybe,' easing the door closed until she moved her delicious foot, 'remember me to inquiring friends.'

'He's on the brink, Walker,' she almost wailed and I said, ' "Daddy" is? Yes, I know.'

'Nolan is, worm. He's on the brink, how do we know what he's crazy enough to do? Unless you know, unless you're double-crossing everybody, honeybun?'

I said anyway didn't I have a double cross coming to me? and she asked me, booming the door, if I had fucked the housekeeper yet which made me mad for complicated reasons and I said—I believe now the seed of it was germinating in my mind while I spelled out the DO NOT DISTURB card, frustrated and wondering if there wasn't some way I could slice into the Doctor's treasured parts and coming up with the strong possibility that Sisterbaby's ghostly but luscious bequests were no less appealing to him than her everyday lusciousness (I've never seen anything like the chubby tight knees of her all but interminable stockings and I doubt if he has)—anyway, I said, 'If Dear Uncle should somehow (you know?) fail to endow you, love, you may find the good medic trying to crawl out the window. Then what, honeybun? What but a life membership in the Unwed Mothers Club (you know?)' perhaps a little involved but she got it. She was swishing up the glass but she swished it down far enough to flip out 'Shithead!' at me like a cigarette butt, revving the motor to smother my answer and cutting up into the Highway the way students throw a Molotov and run.

When I got back to my chair Mr. C had dropped by for a minute.

'. . . you see what he's trying to do, Nolan, I'm sure you do,' the words coming in Nolan's other ear but nobody there either as if old C were showing it wasn't much of a trick if you wanted to bother. 'He's trying to disconcert you, upset your ecology.'

Nolan asked him behind his hand what he should answer but he didn't get much help. 'You figure it out, Nolan, I'm no good at details any more. But I'll say this much, his aim is to destroy us—destroy innocence, decency, uprightness, love, and so destroy us. His craft and power are great——'

'You want 'em destroyed, don't you? for Christ sake! Let me handle it then. It's garbage, Nolan, he can't destroy you without destroying himself. He doesn't know what he wants. Besides, I'm not trying to destroy *you, I'm trying to create you, give you enough rope to hang I should say create yourselves.'*

'You see, Nolan, this spiritual amputee is hoping to cause the young to cast away their one allotted love in profligacy——'

'Hobble off, Stiff, you're dead, go on back to the funeral parlor.'

'——hoping that later their children will have no love to perfect them and the deformed will inherit the earth.'

'Don't swallow all that piss, Nolan.—What about the "deformed" get of real animals, Windbag? Did you ever see one?—Come on, Nolan, let's move round the corner where there's less noise.'

'You're not a "real" animal, Nolan, we've been over that before. You're both creature and creator, creator of the creature with the need and power to create. I have to go now but you might ask him to show you some of the offspring of his degenerates.'

'Nolan, the point is this—now that his bowels have been kind enough to rush him to a celestial shithouse— I'm trying to free you, cut you loose from Old Grandad, give you a chance at something bigger, something better than watching at the bed of a dying parent.'

' "Honor thy father and thy mother——" '

'Oh weeping God!'

Nolan said patiently, 'The trouble with what you're saying is it's not geared to human beings. We need understanding, some tolerance of other people, some kindliness, some give-and-take. Spirit, feeling, heart, religion, those things tell a man how to behave, what's expected of him as a human among humans.'

'That's just it, Nolan, I want you to be SUPER-humans.'

'What you're saying——'

'*Spirit-feeling-heart-religion! Did that help you put a man on the moon? If you'd listened to me sooner you'd be into another solar system by this time.*'

Nolan said surely we had done some good things, we could communicate, had invented tools, had devised intellectual systems, developed ourselves as abstract thinkers, had built a psychic structure raising love out of copulation, spirit out of animalism. 'I'd say on the whole we haven't done badly.'

'*Nolan, if you'll pardon me, you've done as bad as was humanly possible, as bad as you could figure how to do with the stingy handful of breakfast food he gave you for a brain. You see, you've wasted so much time fucking round with this "Experiment" you don't know whether you're good or evil; the question doesn't even occur to a normal healthy animal. What you need, Nolan, if I may make a suggestion, is a relatively simple little operation, much simpler than a hysterectomy but like it in the fact that once you're up and about you're practically indestuctible, a spiritectomy, minor sergery, not even as complicated as that hemorrhoidectomy you had back in the thirties——*'

'*No thank you.*'

'*It's better to take it out like that other appendix, no good to you any more, always likely to start acting up——*'

'*I think you want to strip us down to the level of computers, vending machines stocked with finite answers.*'

'*We're getting off the——*'

'*A computer is just an automatic dead-end, just exhausts the combinations and there you are.*'

'*You've got to know how to program it, Nolan, for Christ sake!*'

*'The combinations are useless unless absorbed by a
man's spirit, by his imagination, his ability to reproduce
generation after generation of more and more complicated ideas. Science just explains, proves, fells the tall
mysteries. A man needs some inner wilderness.'*

'We're getting off the track, Nolan———'

*'Even lumber companies plant seedlings, but you
don't see science planting any dreamlings, as if the
supply of mysteries were inexhaustible. Truth is a fossil
fuel, when you mine up the last of it you freeze from a
lack of questions to warm you———'*

*'Hold it, Nolan. What I'm saying is you're chained
up to that old dead ball in a worse fix than Prometheus,
at least birds were eating out his guts, you're eating
out your own, what the angels leave you, "eagles,"
if you'd rather. I want to cut you free. You've cut a
few of the chains, to be fair with you, but you can't
cut the one that galls you worst of all, not without some
help—how would you like to be free of death, Nolan?
Free of time?'*

The offer must have rocked Nolan because the memory
of it sent his stare into the palms like a blowgun.

*He said he didn't know, and the Voice said, 'Makes
you a little dizzy, doesn't it? Okay, live as long as
you like then, if you're scared to swallow the whole
oyster. Not be a slave to it, not have it laid on your
back every minute like a lash, maybe tonight? maybe
tomorrow? certainly this year? And you know what the
lash is, the cat-o'-nine-tails? It's this God-damned "Experiment" you're being a guinea pig for. It's done
nothing for you but bring you death. Death doesn't
exist for the rest of creation.'*

'*Everything dies.*'

'*Grow up, Nolan! You don't die if you don't see it coming.*'

Nolan said he would have to think about it, and after a minute or two he asked what it would cost him and the Voice chuckled, 'You're smart, Nolan, I knew that as soon as I saw how you hated to part with that quarter of an hour. The price-tag? Not astronomical. You do two or three things for me and it's a deal.'

'*What sort of things?*'

'*Nolan, you fight me like a drowning man, I'm trying to save you!—This sort of thing (I'm a cards-on-the-table man): I've got a few young lostsouls who don't like the way I operate—a vociferous few, I mentioned them to you—dropouts, troublemakers, everybody's got the shingles nowadays, they're saying I'm slow, talk too much and do too little, "too gabby," ought to step down, all that shit. It's time I cracked a few whips, rattled a few pitchforks, you know what I mean? showed them who's who (not pitchforks of course, I don't use them any more, cattle prods are better). I had the big bang all fused and ready to go some years back but you people got scared and let it fizzle out, now it may be ten or fifteen years before it's ready again and I honestly can't afford to wait that long—I'm being frank with you, Nolan, cards down. I'm like Livonia when Stacy and Iona wanted her to postpone the wedding until they could get out from under Christmas: Livonia said, NOW!*'

'*I don't know what you're referring to but——*'

'*Listen, Nolan, I've got a Sixth Column down there in your crowd but you can't trust anybody any more, I need some old-hat reliable mossbacks'll do what they say (not talking about you of course but maybe you've*

*got some friends), and I need a slew of semi-depraveds
for decoys, harder and harder to find the semis——'*

'*You mean Fifth Column.*'

'*Six as in Sextus, a Sexth Column, not time to draw
you a picture, Sex Column if you like. I need more
idleness for it to work on, a one-day week, Nolan, a
no-day week, for Godsake. It's coming but in the mean
time the corporations are making it hard for me, lots
of their people would rather grab a quick profit than
a quick lay, you say, "squeeze," Nolan, and they think
of prices, a price squeeze, profit-and-loss, you say "turn
over" and they think of inventory.' He said many had
already come to feel that women were tedious, expensive
(had been trying to liberate them to get from under the
upkeep), monotonous, often dangerous and sometimes
deadly; the female was losing her pull and if that went
on he was, to speak frankly, up shit creek without a
paddle. He had tried to counteract it by pulling them
out of the kitchen, peeling them down to skin, mixing
them into offices and factories, but it didn't work very
well, not much more screwing than before, among the
children, yes, but the earlier it started the earlier it
petered out and the net gain hardly kept up with inflation. 'I suppose the truth may be, Nolan, there's
always been about as much FPP as they can handle——'*

'*FPP? Those alphabet words!*'

'*Fucks-per-phallus, Nolan, but I'm not willing to
settle for that, backed-up semen is dynamite——'*

'*I'm sorry to be impolite but your language——'*

'*Please, Nolan! I forget about the Gap,' mumbling
other apologies and then going on querulously that he
had tried flooding them with how-to-do-it books and
pictures at about the price of a hamburger, that it seemed
to help at first then everybody started going back to the*

hamburgers. 'I'm ashamed to tell you, Nolan, how many people down there after all I've done are saying, "Come on let's get it over with so I can get some sleep"—heavy day at the office, you see. They have a trick of building up a tolerance against anything you inject them with, I think he's had some of his smartass electricians tie in a sort of circuit-breaker that cuts off at an overload, a sort of fancy governor, did it a long time ago, brought in a swarm of antibodies from one of those reverse galaxies where ass-over-teakettle is the scientific approach——'

Nolan said, 'What's all this got to do with the Experiment?' and he said, 'Simple, Nolan. Get rid of the Experiment and you get rid of old C, the way you get rid of a bothersome reflection by busting the mirror, you understand?'

'I can't say I do.'

'In kindergarten language, Nolan, I'm trying to make you big enough to pull his chair from under him and sit in it yourself, be your own Big Shot. That's a fair deal, isn't it? You don't need faith in God any more, faith in yourself that's what you need.'

'From my observation it looks as if the less we believe in God the less we believe in ourselves, that mixes me up.'

'The trouble is, Nolan, you're trying to do a calculus problem on an abacus——'

'We're uncomfortable—torn apart, indeed!—at the SILENCE of Godlessness. No orders. No suggestions. No reprimands. No Well-dones! Not a sound in the stillness——'

'My God, Nolan, do you want to go on living in a boiler factory?'

'—*no bells on the buoys*, no buoys.'

'*Watch it, Nolan, you're getting off the runway again. The point is I need your help—at a fee of course, I don't expect you to work for nothing. Suppose we run up a fee on your flagpole and see how it waves while we look at some other stuff*, honorarium *rather, sounds bigger, say, a 500-year life.*'

Nolan said cannily he already had a better offer than that and the Voice said, '*Better than that! Oh, I know what you mean. But I'm talking about the real goods, Nolan, in your own body where you can be comfortable, know where everything is, where to find your prick if you need it, not swishing round windy old houses, up and down chimneys, cobwebs, that sort of thing, scaring people, and damn few chimneys that wouldn't land you in an incinerator or a tank of sulphuric acid.*'

He seemed to think Nolan showed a lack of interest because he stepped up the pay. '*Your hallucinema, Nolan, that I put you in the way of——*'

'*He said to leave it alone for now.*'

'*I bet he did! You'd be getting too close to base, that's why. Those moon pictures didn't show you any-thing, but* these, *Nolan, these'll smoke him out. I can lend you a filter'll shoot them in color, widescreen——*'

Nolan said never mind all that, what was the job? what would he be expected to do? and the Voice said, '*Good, Nolan, all right, fair enough—you think I'm gabby, maybe I am—we'd begin with your delightful family.*'

'*Say deceitful, degraded, depraved, degenerate, de-jected, delinquent, despirited—and dispirited too. They're being cast hither and thither and are headed for an evil end.*'

(giving me a widescreen hallucinema flash of myself empty-handed beside a runway watching my pilotless blue Twin-Commanche B take off into the yonder if he felt that way about us).

'You're too hard on them, Nolan. You've got to take your hat off to anything operates the way they do, never a squeak or a rattle, tuned up like a new Rolls. Shows what you can do if you keep your mind on the big things, the belly-and-balls things. All they need is for you to pipe in some fuel. What I would suggest is that you give these people some muscle, some green-back muscle'

(my hair suddenly up on end, no air going in or out of my mouth or nose, almost having to push my eyes back in the sockets)

'so they can carry on with their—but before we go into that, you keep coming back to "evil," Nolan, as if there were something smelly about it. You're all mixed up about evil.'

'Evil is destruction.'

'There you go! What you call evil is just the other half of the cycle, the half in shadow—listen, but there isn't time now. Your family . . .'

'It's getting foggy, Schurz, it's fading out.'

I said, 'Jeepers creepers, Uncle No, don't fade him out yet!' (it sounded as if the Voice were about to solve all our problems in one sweep, Lifetime Exemption, maybe The Home Place, maybe *everything*), Nolan going on, the sweat running down his face, 'Fading out—a lot more but I can't—gone, it's gone,' the words coming out in a whisper or a sigh and Nolan himself seeming to shrink into a whisper or a sigh, gaze resting on the sand at his feet as if it had dropped there with the solid permanent-sounding thump of a nut shaken out of one of the palm trees. 'Cutting us free of God, free of directives however vague, free of purpose—oh, he said, "He's already destroyed you, grabbed his Experiment and run, saving what he could, you've been gutted and don't know it——" '

I said, 'You're going to take the job, aren't you, Uncle Nolan?' but he didn't answer and we watched him, Schurz and I, propping him up with two steady stares, and after a silence he said, turning the telescope eye straight to sea, 'Suppose he's right, Schurz!'

'He's full of shit, Captain, (excuse me).'

'It makes you feel like an astronaut with his sandwich floating off over his head. You don't know which way's up, which way's down. The horizon out there is tilting up to about thirty degrees——'

We caught him as he tried to synchronize with the horizon, walked him between us into the house, Chak holding back the screen door, Mrs. L pattering barefoot ahead of us to shake up the pillows on his slept-in bed.

7

GOD KNOWS WHAT (besides grass and hash and acid, for medicinal purposes) Mollenbrink carries in his black satchel, maybe a few copies of the Manual (for sale) and a few diaphragms, maybe a pair of socks and some dice, but he brought it with him to Nolan's door like a plumber with a tacklebox of wrenches and washers, set it on the fiber rug at the foot of Nolan's bed when he took the chair Mrs. L whisked into place like a registered nurse. Mamma and Sisterbaby tiptoed in and fell on anguished knees at the bedside and Stacy, standing, laid a hand on Nolan's bare shoulder in tight-lipped manly distress—no question but that The Family had arrived, gathered round for The End, Mamma whispering to Mrs. L her status-shaped 'You go on, my dear, we'll take care of him, you must have *loads* to do.' I noticed Stacy had clipped an eager Sign Pen to his shirt pocket, no coats or jackets on the Keys.

Nolan seemed too far gone to notice Mollenbrink tapping about on his chest like a carpenter trying to locate a stud to drive a nail in, propping up his eyelids and squinting all round inside, lifting Nolan's upper lip and reading his gums. I don't think he could remember anything else to do because he began giving us nods at the door to show we were crowding him. When Mrs. L moved to leave with the rest of us

Nolan revived to the extent of bending a bony countermanding wrist at her and Mollenbrink after a second or two gave in.

We shut the door on them but it didn't hurt the accoustics; words too low to come straight through the plywood wriggled easily through chinks and cracks and keyhole, Nolan saying quite audibly, 'I'm just beginning to understand what it was I discovered in my youth,' and Mollenbrink coming in heartily with 'Good, Major!' (I don't know why the boost in grade, maybe his quack way of massaging the patient, stupidity more likely), 'some early masturbating discovery you recalled during the night, I take it?' with a hitching-closer scrape of chair.

Nolan seemed to take a minute to give Mollenbrink the once-over then he said, 'Are we supposed to know this man, my dear?' and 'my dear' said, 'He's your nephew's son-in-law, Captain, no, your nephew-in-law's son, almost son, no——'

'His voice sounds familiar but I never saw him before, would you help him to his hat and coat? we've met all the people we need to know,' Mollenbrink smiling as at a wayward pet (but taking clinical notes of everything—we hoped—for the file) and Nolan continuing, maybe aiming it at Mrs. L, maybe at himself, not apparently at Mollenbrink whom he seemed to have sponged off his slate, 'Good is a line figure, leading on, unlimited. Evil is a hole——'

Mollenbrink said, 'Ah, genitalia!' as if flourishing a gold ingot off the *Señora d'Atocha* out there under the Stream.

'—circular, revolving on itself, dynamic and dangerous but barren, bound in, repetitive. Be careful how you despise an ancient metaphor: Hell underneath and earthbound, Heaven above unlimited in unimaginable space—and many other primitive flashes of truth we are just beginning to see when a modern scope chances on them and the light is strong. "Reveal," in the Biblical sense; "revelation." That is, it was there all along, only in need of being uncovered, not something new but an extension, only our understanding of it new. God is shaping man and man-being-shaped is shaping God——'

'Splendid, Major!'

'—a labor of interacting effort and devotion, of mutual belief in the other's integrity and good faith, an evolution that either one can destroy—how to say it without oversaying it! The chanciness of it, the go-either-wayness! Sunup or sundown. If one of them wavers——'

'Drops his end of the plank! Good! Bonzer!'

'A growing man, a growing God, their fates not yet decided, depending on each other and what they have the capacity to imagine, to glimpse in one of those non-reason flashes we call a bright idea—that is, an idea orbiting a little farther out than reason can reach, in the magnetic field reason will follow into in good time: the Flash, the Idea, the Proof. Perhaps one day we shall be able to imagine what creates the need to imagine, where the need comes from to create at all. We are primitives in an unknown culture——'

'So true, Captain!' (maybe hoping to shut him off by canceling the promotion).

'God will grow as our comprehension grows. And as good becomes more and more good and evil more and more evil perhaps in an instant of mutual perfection they will meet in a collision that will explode into a new galaxy.'

'The Big Bang, ah yes.'

'Good is in the lead,' voice mounting as if he weren't too sure and Mrs. L coming in firmly with 'Captain, I think you should rest now.'

'In a place called The Nine Ways Xerxes took nine of the young men and nine of the maidens and buried them alive at the crossing——'

Mollenbrink said, 'But more recently, Captain, last night in fact, I understand you had a restless night,' and Nolan was suddenly silent at the reminder until in a moment he repeated, 'Last night, last night,' in an end-of-the-world voice.

'Perhaps you would like to tell me about it, Captain?'

Nolan said, By no means, it was too unsettling for words, and Mollenbrink said no possible sexual deviations, depravities, excesses, perversions could be strange to his own ears but if Nolan would feel easier man-to-man perhaps Mrs. Littleberry would be so good as to busy herself outside for a few minutes, to which Nolan answered, 'Don't move, my dear,' and after a few seconds went on, 'The Experiment—last night something told me,' fumbling for words to fit, 'a voice said to me—the Experiment is the chain—that chains us,' pausing as if unable to shape it, at which Mollenbrink broke in, 'Speaking of experiments, sir, I have a little book here, my own by chance—$7.95——'

'The guiding belief of my life, and my fathers' lives before me, my rudder,' mumbling on, gaze on the ceiling as if sorting out the night for himself alone, 'was that there was a Purpose—and the Purpose was to promote the growth, the evolution, not of man but of the spirit of man, to erect on man the animal——'

'Erection!'

'—an ever-growing, ever-expanding——'

'Jesus peezus, Captain! Wish I'd been there——'

'*Enough, enough!*' Mrs. L cried out in a voice magnified from the one she had used in the yard for 'Enough of old!' but Nolan wasn't a man for screeching to a stop.

'The voice, according to the voice, this Purpose is only a swindle, something like, like the blindfold we tied on the mule at the cane press in the country, to keep him plodding on his round-and-round. This voice—I had believed the state of man's spirit now was only dormant, only deep in a re-

fueling sleep, but suppose it is not a sleep? Suppose the real Purpose is to free ourselves of spirit? Or suppose there is *no* Purpose? And sunup's really sundown?—I felt the way I did a few years ago when a high wind out of Puerto Rico took the roof from over me.'

'*Orgasm*, Captain! Wonderful! The lid blowing off, release, freedom.'

'My house was in ruins, my books, my work, my thought. All I had left was spirit——'

Mrs. L cried, 'Enough of spirit! You must rest now,' but Mollenbrink went on with the joys of true freedom, 'freed of superstition, of guilt, shame, worry, unhappiness, of love (so-called), of so-called poetry, freed of good and evil——'

Nolan said it sounded like what we had been on all-fours and Mrs. L went up the wall: 'All-fives! All-sixes! He's got to rest now, Doctor!'

I had pulled Stacy away from his turn at the keyhole to tell him I thought Nolan needed an MD more than an SOB but I didn't get to say it. Nolan's first 'Doctor' carried a sort of question mark after it but his second was a straight-out '*Doctor!*' that shook the plywood. It may be he reached for something, the hourglass, the chamberpot, but *Doctor!* was followed by a scramble of noises that included what might have been an overturning chair (Mollenbrink's), a thump that could have been Mollenbrink's tacklebox against a bed-post or the bureau, uneven footsteps (stomps, rather) and the rattle of the knob as Mollenbrink flung back the door from our noses and ears and burst out with a hissing, 'Seven shits! He's for the cage.'

I felt like needling him and I asked if he wouldn't diagnose everybody's sudden obsession with 'shit' as a symptom of mass constipation, or mass diarrhea. 'Or certainly a mass gastro-intestinal tract not happy with the problem,' (I got the idea of the unhappy g-i tract from being round Stacy so much, who could hardly ever rise from a chair without such rumblings and grunts and finally hissings and fizzings as to pass for any backhouse words in the language).

'He's for the cage, and put her in with him.'

I added, 'Or certainly an anal fixation of some sort,' and he interrupted his diagnosis long enough to spit out, 'Let me do the fixations, Walker, if you will!' going on with bedside details we already knew, Stacy leading us all out to a family consultation in the yard and a Professional Opinion (caps) from Mollenbrink that Nolan was in no legally responsible mental condition to draw up a menu lot less a new will—which sparked several satisfied nods from us, theirs based on the hope this would leave Mrs. L shivering out in the cold and mine on the belief he had written the existing will in pre-Dudo days and had done the decent thing (I hadn't had a chance to tell them Dudo had stabbed them in the back, us).

Stacy cut it short with three all-rights and a get-to-the-point, which was how to deliver 'him' to the judge's office 'today, right now, he may be better tomorrow, there's your car, Leon—or maybe it's mine, I'm buying it—put him in, we can have him there in an hour.'

Mollenbrink said with some extra-professional starchiness he wouldn't consent to moving his patient now. 'Tomorrow, tomorrow morning'; he said he would feed him a double dose of tablets that would take his mind off the housekeeper long enough to get a good night's sleep, and Stacy said, 'You don't have to put him in shape to run the Belmont Stakes, Leon, for Christsake,' but he ended by accepting tomorrow, said he would phone the judge and set it up for eleven, pausing a minute to change gears then wading in considerably deeper by asking in a by-the-way tone that didn't fool anybody if Mollenbrink could recommend some nice bin, not too expensive. (I was annoyed at the way they were bypassing me and my plan, Chak all primed and ready to go, but I could see this last nightmare had pushed Nolan farther along the bin-trail than if Chak had shaken him all night and not let him have it; anyway, you don't turn down the sugar because it's not your spoon.) Mollenbrink said cautiously there were 'several excellent sanatoria' (holding back on names until he could discuss kickbacks with managers), at which Mamma as next of kin squeezed out a few slow tears that the wind brushed off.

A brief and cryptic exchange occurred at the open door of the Bug when Stacy, who had probably been thinking about Mollenbrink's bill-or-no-bill since his own 'not too expensive'—if he hadn't been thinking about it all night— brought up the fee business again in another by-the-way put-on as he prepared to crumple himself into the driver's seat. He said he thought we could hold her in the road from here on in, certainly after tomorrow's rap with the Judge, and we weren't going to let Leon sacrifice any more of his time on free-loading in-laws, not with an officeful of paying patients waiting for him at home (mothers with children usually, taking the 'Child-Guidance' bait, the Doctor more interested in the mammas than the children).

Mollenbrink lifted a magnanimous hand to accompany a magnanimous 'Let's not worry about that, shall we? hhm?' Sisterbaby gliding between him and me and on some inscrutable (to me) prehistoric female whimsy sticking a hand in my pants pocket which I hadn't the guts to shake loose from. Stacy's worry wasn't so easily cured though, indeed the gentle 'hhm?' seemed to strike him like the needle injecting the anesthetic, quite a little jab in itself but also suggesting that's not the end of it. He said, the steering wheel against his chin by then (the VW was at least a size and a half too small), 'Just so we won't be screwing around in the dark, Leon, maybe you could give me a general idea what your tab ought to look like,' (clear enough from his choice of words his unconscious was trying to tell him he was screwed already but didn't want to admit it), and Mollenbrink said, lifting the upper pink lip in homage to the coming pleasantry, 'What's the matter with screwing round in the dark?' all of it interrupted by Mamma's batting at a Pelican lizard on the windshield and muttering, 'Get her out of here.'

Stacy said, 'Who, lamb?'—of course he knew but he needed a second to lay down the bill matter, and Mamma said, *'Get her out!'*

'But *how*, tumblebun? That's where the soreness is.'

'Kidnap her.'

'Oh now, wait a minute——'

Sisterbaby said, 'Right, Mamma! Snatch her.'

Stacy said he couldn't do that, he was going to be elected secretary Kiwanis Club next week if he lived that long and Sisterbaby said, 'Don't be such a mossballs, Daddy,' nuzzling the other hip against Mollenbrink to test my circuits— and Mollenbrink's—(it had marched in a Freedom-of-Exposure demo at the University when some mossballs in the Dean's Office tried to make an issue of her bare tits on the cover of *Evergreen Review*—neither here nor there, I believe I mentioned it anyhow), at which Mollenbrink led her to the Continental and Stacy cranked up the Bug, smothering the conference—already half smothered by the familiar-sounding cylinders of Suzuki 750 tilting off the Highway and coughing a little on the down slope, the passenger on the rumble this time an ancient man in a Sears-Roebuck shirt and Levi's with two ropes of white hair partly wrapped with what looked like red-and-black typewriter ribbon. His face was wrinkled like a brown relief map of the Rocky Mountains (the only person I've ever seen whose head looked as if it had already been to a shrink); Nolan was a teenager beside him, Chak as proud of him as if he had been the

ghost of a U.S. President: 'Grandpa Chak, ladies and gentlemen, Chak the Fifth, I'm Chak the Seventh. Brought him
to see the Captain. Grandpa's our medic,' Grandpa as grave
to our bows-and-smiles as if he had looked in the eye of a
hundred hurricanes and thought there might be others. (I
don't think 'medic to see Nolan' penetrated or they would
all have piled out again; as it was, ready to leave, thinking
elsewhere, they were up the slope and gone before the
Chaks reached the house.)

In the bedroom Mrs. L was telling Nolan from the
window, 'They've gone,' Nolan answering with a grumbled
two or three words I didn't catch but that might well have
been we hadn't gone far enough, continuing with he didn't
know how he was going to get rid of us, Dudo had been a
big disappointment to him (all of it framed in the Moorish
keyhole-view that reminded me of one of Mamma's wish-
you-were-heres from the Alhambra—she didn't any such
thing; Chak was evidently showing Grandpa the bathroom
before bringing him to his patient). 'In the mean time, keep
away from them, please, my dear—don't ask me to explain.'

Mrs. L said she understood (as you might say, All right,
or, If you say so) but Nolan had to read more into it: 'You
understand?' fixing her with the good eye as though trying
to decide if her wireless had picked up something his hadn't,
Mrs. L saying briskly to the window curtains, 'Quiet now,
time for sleep.'

Nolan lay there silent for a minute staring at the ceiling
as if listening to her closing the venetian blinds, ping after
ping, then he said, like somebody swimming underwater and
coming up where you didn't expect, (I heard it—with ears
I'd have thought were ready by then for anything), 'The
wires to God are down.' She pinged the last one shut as if
to stop him but it didn't. 'The line is cut. We are free. Free

of ropes to grasp, of rails to hold to, of a lee quarter out of the wind——'

'Enough! Sleep first, talk second.'

'What's to quiet a man's terror at seeing himself no longer a part of the enfolding whole?'

When I got back from moving down the hall to make way for Chak and Grandpa, What's-her-name the cat slithering in the door with them between their feet, he was back on the relatively simpler question of how to get rid of us, putting it to Chak and Grandpa in spite of Mrs. L's insistence he must sleep now, they could only stay a second, Chak near the bed and translating for Grandpa farther away and circling flat hands in the space between him and Nolan (not translating from another language but from a nearly toothless American language that nobobdy else seemed able to untangle).

'What's that, Grandpa?'

'Gumble lumble derumble oatmeal uranium.'

'He says, "Getting rid of them's no problem," Captain.'

Nolan said, No problem! Well, *how*, for goodness sake? and Grandpa said, 'Bumble saloon car nutcracker, tea coffee demilk horse pistol.'

'He says it's like the turtles way out on Three Turtles.'

'The Dry Tortugas? dear me! Ask him if he knows Dr. Mudd,' Mrs. L whispering, 'Quiet now,' hand on his chest as he seemed about to get up.

Grandpa ran on for a few seconds which Chak translated as, 'Never mind Dr. Mudd. He says he's talking about big turtles getting rid of little turtles.' Nolan said, 'All right, all right, tell him to go on,' and Grandpa rumbled-bumbled for a minute glancing at a window and the door as if undecided which was the best way out.

'What does he say, Chak?'

'He says, "If turtlets don't want to leave turtle, turtle leaves turtlets," '—which stopped the reel, everybody frozen in a single frame, or at least Nolan and Mrs. L; then the reel running again with Nolan moving his bony shanks out of bed and Mrs. L discouraging him and Nolan saying, 'Stock the boat, Chak.'

'On your side now, you're going to sleep.'

'Will do, Captain. Soon as I put Grandpa back. Come on, Grandpa.'

'Check the water, check the gas, check the tires——'

'Quiet now!'

'The closer you base your values on sub specie aeternitatis the closer you come to despair—because you know such a small fraction of aeternitatis.'

'QUIET! Sleep now! Sleep. One—two—three—sleep.'

And he did. So help me, she rubbed his left ear (the up one) and erased him like a pencil mark; he was gone immediately, beginning to say, 'Get hold of Schurz to—bring—bring . . . .' and not finishing for eighteen hours, Mrs. L skittering about barefoot all day, finger on lips if I took a deep breath (from noon on, the place was like a funeral parlor), then, about sunset, stretching out beside him on the bed until the sun was rising out of the Gulf Stream aiming down the Highway hell-bent for Key West, when he went on, '. . . to bring the birds aboard—what's the sun doing over there?'

8

I HAD A DREAM MYSELF (as who wouldn't, for pity's sake), I was flying so fast—on my own, not the usual thing—I overhauled the blue-and-white Twin Comanche B as she tried to escape me with an Immelmann turn into a tropical disturbance over the Virgin Islands and crawled up on the tail fins trying to find the hand brake, all of it carrying such an obviously personalized directive I decided in the middle of the night I would talk to Nolan at breakfast, or right after if 'my dear' was underfoot, and de-kin myself from the rest by dropping enough hints to warn him away from Key West and the Judge's office, in return for which he could reward me to whatever extent he felt became him.

When I opened my eyes and sniffed for coffee or bacon or biscuits or sausage or pancakes and drew in nothing but shrimp and barnacles and mud flats at rotten low tide I still couldn't believe anything was up and I called out of my door at the kitchen to put 'em on I'd be there in half a minute (I almost said half a pee but remembered where I was). Then at the bathroom window I noticed something wrong with the dock, something hatless or roofless or topless about it like a building lot with a bulldozed tree that had always been there, and it penetrated at last the *Mudd* was gone—and not just gone, not just moored farther out in the Cove, but nowhere in sight, or hearing either though I listened

120

for a full open-mouthed minute before diving at the phone in the hall and on the way kicking the note I hadn't seen on the floor: *'If you must go before we return'* (Mrs. L's hand I should say but clearly Nolan's accent) *'lock doors, leave keys at Gift Shop. N.B.'*—quite a coating of frost I thought on the 'N.B.' instead of 'Uncle' or 'Nolan' or even 'Cordially, N.B.' I dialed Schurz naked as I was, the tube halfway to the floor in sympathetic dejection.

Yes, 'they' had gone on a little cruise.

'Cruise, Mr. Schurz?' And he elaborated: Longboat for gas, Key West, The Dry Tortugas (for a how-do-you-do no doubt to Grandpa's three turtles), Fort Jefferson (and howdy to Dr. Mudd), Nolan, Helga my dear, Chak, Delia and three of Schurz's upper-crust pigeons (Big Blue, Jake, Sue Red) in an upper-crust carrying basket which would be opened on the parade ground at the Fort, timing the 'toss' to a split second on Nolan's watch (synchronized with Schurz's) for the pigeons' resumé——

I shouted it was a hell of a smartass way to treat a house-guest and Schurz started in on 'The Captain sets his own example.'

'I realize that but——'

'Law unto himself, I remember once . . .' et cetera, et cetera. (I had seen Chak and Mrs. L rattling round on board but I thought they were tuning up for a little outing and boat ride in which I would certainly be included, no part of a turtlet.)

Stacy jumped clean out of the telephone when I got to him like the gook out of Aladdin's lamp. 'Gone! He couldn't be gone we're taking him to KW in half an hour.' I said just the same he was gone and Stacy started over it again, stammering back the ports of call when I named them, in fact stammering back everything I said until he more or less got his balance with 'Crazy as a June bug, proves it, like I told you all along!' and finally showed he was on both his flat feet with 'What did you just sit there picking your nose and let it happen for, Walker?'

I tried to say I couldn't tell what was in Nolan's mind, who could? 'I didn't think he would——'

'Didn't think, didn't think! But there's somebody over there knows her ass from a hole in the ground, or was— I'm not talking about you, Walker—somebody knows where to find a hungry justice-of-the-peace, or maybe a hungry preacher if she's got to have it in a church with bells. You gotta get on that boat, Walker.' I said how could I possibly get on the boat? and he said, 'That's your little red wagon.'

I wanted to tell him he was neck and neck with Nolan on the bin-road but I just played along. 'You going to buy me a speedboat to catch them with?' thinking the 'buy' would stop him, and it did slow him down enough for me to say, 'And what would I do if I got on? besides throw up,' (I don't sail well). He said, 'You'd bring him to the courthouse to the Judge, Walker, where've you been all week? how are you going to bin somebody if you can't find him?' quieting then like a motor with the choke coming unstuck and saying, 'Be out in front in five minutes,' and hanging up.

They hunched over while I stuffed myself in the back seat, Stacy and Mollenbrink in the VW, (nobody back there where a flash dream had told me Sisterbaby was hiding on the floor with her skirts pulled up though it was too close to start anything much anyway—Mollenbrink with blue-green gratification tires hanging down beneath his one-way sunglasses). We checked the pump at the Longboat Marina— they had never heard of the *Samuel A. Mudd*—did a U whip-around on the dock and set off rat-tat-tatting over the stream of consciousness bridges and, nearly noon by then, rat-tat-tatted into a sweat-soaked parking slot by the Monroe County (Key West) Courthouse.

It had taken me a while to get the picture, Stacy uncommunicative, 'playing it by ear' (of course), but I think he also just didn't want to talk about it. I had said when I fell into the car if this was a snatch they could drop me off at the *Red Man's* because I had a nervous stomach and he said to cool it. I said, 'Well, what *is* it all about then? If you don't mind.'

'It's about keeping this Nazi fluff out of the J.P.'s front parlor, Walker, it's about stopping her from crawling off with your mother's inheritance, or sailing off with it, not to mention your own foothold on the corner of Easy Street and Featherbed Lane and your sister Livonia's, if that answers your question.'

I said if they were so bent on getting married I didn't see how he could stop them they were both of age, Nolan particularly, and he said, 'Diagram it, Leon,' turning back to the straightaway bridges that made you think you were on water skis on a glassy sea, gulls circling, horizon all round (hazy), a few boats out but nothing that looked like the *Samuel A. Mudd.* The diagram seemed to show that one had trouble getting a marriage license if one were headed for the bin and we as members of the patient's family and attending physician were aiming at beating the happy pair to the Judge's chambers (where they kept the mariage licenses) to obtain commitment papers, 'a mittimus,' says Mollenbrink from above, 'for an aged relative mentally ill to the extent of possibly harming himself and others.'

'If Judge won't sign it without Exhibit A himself,' Stacy said for his own ears, 'and *you* can't round him up,' for mine, 'she'll have his name and won't sign his marriage license either,' (the Judge was female, liberated from long peonage).

I pointed out he didn't have to have a marriage license to sneak off to the bankbox and change the will, or hand over his $30,000 Lifetime Exemption, but it sounded from what they said as if a mittimus was a stop-payment on practically anything Nolan put his pen to after the Judge signed it, codicils, LEs, checks, everything. Anyhow they weren't worried, as long as we could outrun him to the courthouse, which of course we could if he didn't have too much of a lead on us.

The Judge had gone to dinner and we consulted for a while in the sticky hall whether to tour the waterfront looking for Nolan (nobody had seen anything resembling the pair at the courthouse) and maybe lose time with the Judge if she woke up and got back early, maybe have somebody get in to see her ahead of us—*Nolan maybe* (Mollenbrink's morbid idea), 'he might just walk in the door, you don't know where he is'—or to wait for Her Honor there at the courthouse.

We split up. Stacy said, 'Take the car, Walker, see if you can find him, if you can, bring him right on here in the car if you can find him,' very uptight, Mollenbrink giving him a professional gaze over the sunglasses measuring him for being comfortable on the couch. I tried to tell him Nolan set his own example, how was I going to persuade him to come get in the car, in the bin indeed? even a dogcatcher had a net, Stacy going right on with 'Try Garrison Bight he may be tied up there; if he is—no, hold it, go straight to the bank, Florida First National, you may find him in the vault doing things to the will, find both of them, red-handed.' I made the mistake of saying we didn't know whether Nolan had a box at the Florida First National, or anywhere else, and he said, 'Find out, Walker! Find out! Do I have to hold you by the hand?'—sometimes I think I'll go in business for myself, or used to think so.

I made three stops before the blow fell, the Bight, the Bank and Pete's—blows began to fall I should say because they kept falling one on top of the other for four days until we felt like the jack rabbits you see Western farmers on TV beating with sticks or the harmless young seals that trappers in the Arctic beat down; five days, counting Stacy's beating when he finally cornered Mollenbrink and was slammed with some details about the bill, a Saturday I believe but it may have been Sunday, the time-clutch wasn't holding right: 'OV and expenses,' says Mollenbrink twiddling a joint, assuming we could make the translation (OV to Office Visit), 'we'll let it go at that.'

Stacy asked him how he meant, let it go at that, and Mollenbrink took a deep breath and went on patiently that actually all this ought to be figured at HC rates (House-Call, what else? it certainly wasn't OV) which naturally carried a bit more burn but under the circumstances, Livonia, family, and all that, we'd let it ride on OV, the usual ninety-five an hour. 'I don't mean I'd stick you for the full twenty-four hours, just a normal eight-hour day.'

'Just a normal eight-times-ninety-five day! Good God, Leon, that's—what's that, Walker?—that's—' (and when I got out my fingers and told him) 'that's seven hundred and sixty dollars a day!' I felt sorry for him, with all that had gone before by then, bled white already (though the rest of us were just as white); I could see his fingers working as he tried to multiply seven hundred and sixty by the number of days since Mollenbrink had left his office then pitching in a lump sum for the *Ship-n-Shore* and the airlines and the Rent-a-Car people. He didn't seem to hear Mollenbrink's sporty concession as to leaving Saturday and Sunday at the weekday rate, 'I'm not going to bump you for overtime,' it was cruel—but this is getting ahead of myself, who am on my way to Garrison Bight (postponing the Bank for no good reason except that I knew the way to the Bight, throwing my weightlessness around).

Even so, in three quarters of an hour I had checked all the docks and pumps I could locate, with no news of the *Samuel A. Mudd* or crew and was feeding a meter at the Bank thinking of the drunk (I always do) who bought an hour and said, 'My God, I've lost a hundred pounds!' (I was feeling good—everything not perfect but we had beat them to the courthouse which pretty certainly washed out Mrs. L as surviving spouse).

Inside, the place felt like a tank of slightly-discolored female porpoises, the girls all in lavender uniforms with lavender eyelids lifted at the clock creeping on to closing time as if it were about to throw them a tasty smelt. I asked the one swimming about a desk in front of the locks and bolts and bars of the vault if Mr. Nolan Bennett had a box there—I could see somebody in the vault but it wasn't Nolan and Nolan wasn't in the main tank either, I had already looked. She said, 'We don't reveal such information,' as wide-eyed as if I had reached for one of them. I said it was all right to tell me, Mr. Bennett was my uncle, we thought he had a box there, the family did, but we weren't sure, we thought he had said it was this bank but he was old and didn't speak very clearly, and she clamped her porpoise jaws and said she wasn't permitted to divulge information concerning box-holders, tacking on a finalizing 'sir.'

It looked like the end but I said, 'I'm not trying to *get in* your box, Betty baby,' (I didn't mean it the way it sounded—meant 'your' in the sense of you-all's, you-and-the-bank's—no time for that sort of thing right then with the two sweating back at the courthouse and the Nolan-box problem still up, but she seemed to take no, do we say? umbrage, in fact lowered both lavender eyelids for a propitious second); 'I just want to know if he *has* a box, so I won't have to go all over town looking for it every which way.'

She said the Bank would have to have Mr. Bennett's authority before she could answer any questions, would I care to speak to one of the officers? phone about to go into the neck joint where my nose ought to have been and I started calling on some of the craftiness Vidrine & Birlant paid me so miserably for, saying, 'No thank you,' and adding carelessly, 'If he gives me a letter you'll know his signature, I suppose?' She said, Oh yes it would be on file, and rather pleased with myself I thanked her and crossed the street to a show window labeled *'Pete's'* with an overflowing seidel of beer painted on the glass (my third and last stop); it would have been a gamble but I would have given two-to-one she also hadn't seen Mr. Bennett lately, ten-to-one not today— and in twelve minutes Mr. Bennett wouldn't be able to get in.

Pete's seemed built especially for bugging the Bank doors for twelve minutes and I pushed in, a dim rectangular hideaway from a now somehow jaundiced sunshine, TV busted but the radio chattering exuberantly in those endless and halfway consoling inanities that make you feel smarter than everybody else, remind you after a few swallows (me rather) of organ-grinder men and foot-high somersaulting monkeys, the tables mostly empty when—twelve minutes gone and no Nolan—I decided to have my beer sitting down measuring the lunch-break girls through the window. It was all loud and confident and cozy, the radio and various other sounds of Marching-On civilization, hums of air conditioner, fridge motor, and now and then the automatic cut-in of the motor watching over the pressure in the kegs. I ordered up another seidel, letting one dreamy ear pick out some phrases here and there from Freddy Forecast while I tried to look down the waitress's collar when she brought it, tidily wiping off the table, '. . . an Air Force reconnaissance plane sent out to scout the area reported winds of thirty to forty miles per hour in gusts . . .' and I turned away to paying for the beer (a short-term-credit place).

By the time I got back to watching the sidewalk-girls Freddy was saying, 'According to a Miami Weather Bureau storm advisory,' and I gave him more than one ear, not quite two. I missed something and picked him up again at '. . . season's eighth non-tropical low-pressure system, unlike Gilda, is pinpointed in the Caribbean about a hundred miles east-southeast of Yucatan . . .' and I put down a good swag of the beer, a local brew I don't know the name of.

Then he said, '. . . small craft warning . . .' and I gave him both ears because it cleared up so many questions: Nolan wasn't in Key West at all. Hadn't been here. Had picked up the warning from an earlier Freddy on the *Mudd's* shortwave and put about for home—sidestepped our tackle as we moved in to nail him, Stacy would have said on happier afternoons.

Then, distinctly, '. . . Helga is moving slowly north-east——'

'Helga?'

'—at about fifteen miles per——'

'HELGA!' I started getting up, as if that would change anything.

'—and is expected to pass west of the Florida Keys some-time early tomorrow morning——'

'HELGA!'

The waitress skipped in and said her name was Janice, please, everybody looking at me standing up, or my hair, or both of us. There was something about it like the two images you catch in a night-driving mirror, the two pictures in a windowpane, one beyond, one behind, and both of them right there, something like a quick handshake from a double-ganger—all of it righting itself at once and leaving me with the foot-on-the-ground consideration that 'small craft warning' certainly included Volkswagens and it was time to head the hell out of Key West, out of Pelican too, out of the whole sunup-sundown keychain of them.—I squeezed through the street door just ahead of Pete and a Cuban helper hauling out some experienced-looking shutters to the front for the window with the seidel of beer.

Stacy was pacing the sidewalk at the courthouse like a grocery-clerk sentry in the National Guard, Mollenbrink snoozing on a bench under a royal palm (at ninety-five an hour, though we didn't know the rate then). I squeaked into the Sheriff's slot, squeaking, 'Pile it in!'

He said, 'Where you been, son, all this time, you smell like Milwaukee?' and I said, 'Tell you as we go,' dealing with his annoyance by throwing, at him my win at the Bank: 'He's got a box at the First National but he hasn't been there today.' 'You sure?' 'I'm sure, and the reason he hasn't is he's turned round and gone home which is what we better the hell do too, there's a wind coming, she's on the radio, and her name——'

'Wind? Big wind? Get in the back!—*LEON!* Look at that bastard dead on my time' (little did he know) . . . .

They were talking about 'papers' as we headed out, hurricane-stained shutters going up on Market Street—the *Petition for Commitment* papers, which they had signed, and the mittimus, which the Judge wouldn't sign without Nolan: 'The patient is required to appear,' says she. 'Yes ma'am,' says Stacy (probably Leon too). 'The Court fixes a hearing one week from today at ten-fifteen a. m.,' somehow aiming her eyes at them one eye to each as if they had been a pair of bloodhounds sent to turn her back to the old slave quarters; 'Does the ill person have an attorney?' 'No ma'am, we didn't think——' 'The Court appoints J. Suarez of Suarez & Kirzl to represent the patient, next case,' with a rap of knuckle on desk and a nod to Ashalom's big-eared aunt.— Mollenbrink said in the car he had an idea the J stood for Juanita, trying to give the impression he couldn't wait to lay hands on her but I think he and Stacy were really both glad they had a week's leeway.

Near the edge of town, the sunlight already fading into a sort of seasick green, we passed a boy-young-man on the sidewalk with tarbrush hair smoking a cigar and picking out what looked like pineapples and limes at an outdoor fruit-stand. Before I could think fast enough to keep my mouth shut I said, 'That couldn't be Chak, could it? that boy with the basket, Nolan's boy,'—what did it matter if it was? too late to run down Nolan and take him to the Judge today even if Stacy and Mollenbrink had the backbone to do it with a hearing set for next week (or the backbone to face her again at all); I was only laying myself open to attack for having missed him (he had probably chugged in after I left the Bight—if he *was* in KW). I said, 'No, it couldn't be Chak, go on, go on,' because Stacy was pulling in to the curb, whoever it was two short blocks back by then, clouds of Hav-A-Tampa round his head like cauliflowers.

It was there in our minute or two at the curb that we lived through the nice problem—each of us simultane-ously—of how to appear to be persuaded by somebody to do something you are already persuaded to do but want some-body else to be at the bottom of, in this case what to do about Chak, by which we meant Nolan, or rather Nolan-and-the-wind ('Nolan-and-Helga' would be confusing). We talked about them for a time, saying one thing and thinking some-thing else (Stacy left the motor running out of respect for the imminence of a solution), *saying*, of course Nolan would tie up at KW until it blew out, no call for us to do anything, not even sure the boy was Chak, and what could we do any-way? and *thinking* (hardly daring to think it), if everybody kept real still now, held his breath with all his fingers crossed, it might just turn out to be the ill wind we had been waiting for, talking about the situation and the five of them (Delia and Mudd in it too by then) from various carefully screened hide-outs until Mollenbrink brought it all out into the open with 'Do we really have any right to bother him?' (quite comfortable now among the heirs), 'I mean, really now, a man's entitled to do his screwing in private if that's the way he wants it, isn't he? hmm?' covering in his gaze-about all the family problems, large, small, medium, that might be on the very brink of solution if Nolan simply by the grace of God disappeared. Stacy asked me if I honestly thought it could be the boy (wanting me in a little deeper, as if I hadn't already said it couldn't be once), and I said I didn't see how it could possible be, Nolan would long ago have headed for home, might be there by now—all three of us watching the boy go round a corner (a calico cat on his shoulder now, I'm sorry to say)—and Stacy let in the clutch.

Pelican was pitch dark when we got there though the sun was hardly down, no wind but a mean sort of edgy something in the air like a badly sharpened knife, or a knife being badly sharpened, like Mamma with her nose out-of-joint, no *Samuel A. Mudd* at the dock yet when we swung down into the yard for a minute to be sure. I said, 'Not yet,' giving the humid darkness my seaman's scan to the west, sou'west, nor'west, and Stacy said, 'Tied up at KW, naturally,' the prayer that Nolan had headed out for Yucatan as a welcoming committee on his face like sweat. Mollenbrink said, 'Hhm,' (playing it both ways until he could be sure).

We got through the God-damned gale intact, no bones broken, whatever her name was—doors blown off hinges, gutters off houses, tin roofs rolled up like joints, fish on the Highway, shingles in the sky like machetes, six inches of water in Dudo's office, lobster trap in a palm tree, trees like picked chickens, a corner of the *Ship-n-Shore* No-Vacancy sign showing in the Cove like a surfacing diver.

It didn't bother us much, locked up tight in 17 with the window boarded up (heart-shaped air-hole in the center board, used lumber no doubt) except we began to worry, about daylight, there wasn't going to be enough stuff in Mollenbrink's medicine bag to see us through, the wind out there like a thousand-car freight train on a trestle and us under it. When the last car whipped over and we looked out almost stunned by the sudden silence (it must have been close to noon and must have been Wednesday, I'm not sure about the day of the week) the place seemed to be in the state I was in after the rear-strangle-hold-and-take-down of a DI I once knew, standing back from me, finger-thumb arc at the belt—'Get on your feet, young man.' 'You going to knock me down again, sir, Sergeant?' '*Knock you down?* Don't you know a DI can't touch a trainee, I'm showing you an exercise.'

All the 'natives'—Dudo, Schurz, Mrs. Maple, Ashalom— more or less agreed with the DI, Helga hadn't hit us, was just passing by on an exercise to the west of us. But the point was (when we got the sand and seaweed and shrimp and fishbones out of one of the cars and could make our way to Nolan's empty dock), where was the *Samuel A. Mudd?*— giving each other a sort of consolatory dead eye as we stood there in the sand and watched to see who would be the first to admit that the real point (unless she *was* at KW) was where was what is known as the Last Will and Testament? In the box at the Florida First we didn't doubt, or wouldn't have doubted if we had been low enough to word the question, but we didn't actually know.

As for the boat and 'all hands,' the authorities were concerned in their own way: the Marine Patrol was out full force, CG cutters frisked among the reefs and shoals, choppers chopped, scout planes banked and stitched and circled over every square yard of land and water from the Marquesas to Fort Jefferson—fewer day by day, and the bulletins fewer, until there it came, in a resinous brown squawk out of Ashalom's instrument panel as we talked in a spot of shade at the *Ship-n-Shore* watching Dudo shovel Gulf sand out of the swimming pool (Ashalom was apparently convinced the whole disappearance was somehow an inside job but needed a little more before he was ready to take us before the DA)—'*The Samuel A. Mudd, Pelican, missing for three days, is presumed lost with all hands.*'

I stood in the door of 18 where they were all gathered (17 was being aired) and recited it word for word to the bereaved family, 'Florida First National' coming out of our eyes.

We could hardly find our way to Key West through the tears, Mollenbrink at the dreamboat controls of the Continental with Sisterbaby beside him (*against* him, and with her left hand God knows where), Stacy and I in the back with Mamma between us, tears that reminded me of Nolan's reminiscing about watering the stock down on the farm when he was a boy, how you primed and pumped and primed and pumped until your shoulder was out of joint and the leathers finally caught and out it gushed; at one gush from Mamma I told Sisterbaby to start the wipers, which brought me a flock of icicle stares and doubled the gush-content. Red-eyed and sniffling we tracked down J. Suarez (brunet, no beard but moustache coming along, hair on her chest—a guess but Mollenbrink had lost no time in mumbling 'Dyke'—not 'Juanita' but 'Juliana' if that matters, which it doesn't), and red-eyed and sniffling and in the presence of a junior bank official and the lock-box girl (sorry now for the way she had treated me), plus Madam Suarez and a Court Order, watched the locksmith bore out the lock.

It was there all right, on top of everything (newly-arrived, it suddenly occurred to me) and Suarez grabbed it ahead of Stacy like a contraband Cuban cigar and put it in her jacket pocket. We tried to look in at what smelled like a load of triple-A-gilt-edged blue chips but the bank man held us back three or four feet as if we were trying to jump off a cliff— which if there had been a cliff he might as well have been kind enough to let us jump off of.

We were given the complete breakdown in the Judge's office, chairs in a semicircle for the family (courtesy of Ashalom's aunt), an extra semicircle behind for Schurz and Mrs. Maple as witnesses to Dear Uncle's hand and seal and Suarez as Friend of the Court or simple busybody (at a percentage-of-gross fee), past lunchtime by then and all of us so uptight (the 'heirs,' I mean, quote unquote, I don't speak for the back row) our insides sounded like a tribe of mice in the attic:

'. . . *is the desire of the party of the first part, through the means of the trust created under the terms and provisions of this instrument . . .'* (the Judge taking her time, sadist at heart) '. . . *and by these presents does hereby give, grant and convey to the said Trustee that parcel of land known as THE HOME PLACE, comprising twenty-seven and six-tenths (27.6) acres more or less, and more particularly described under ITEM IV of this instrument, to be administered as a Bird Sanctuary——'* (Stacy said, 'Read that again!' the Judge not even shifting focals to give two raps on desk) '. . . *as well as that parcel of land known as BENNETT'S FOLLY, lying upon the Savannah River in the State of Georgia and more particularly described . . .'*

The old bastard had set up a foundation with the bank at home as trustee, The Nolan Bennett Foundation. Everything went into it, even Great-grandpa Bennett's hunting-case watch and chain, The Home Place to be operated as a Bird Sanctuary ('I can't stand it!' Mamma said; Mollenbrink walked out of chambers with 'If Your Honor please, I must go piss on something') and the Folly land to be *held in perpetuity as a Wildlife Refuge for the comfort and wellbeing of any of the more promising quadrapeds, bipeds and plants*' that Mr. C might care to station there (no doubt for Experimental purposes—basic-training—deemed by the Testator too complicated to explain).

Sisterbaby and Mrs. Maple assisted Mamma to the sofa in the Ladies', Madam Suarez assisting as far as the door but seeming hesitant about going in.

As Stacy and I, speechless, speech sucked out of us, were moving to join Mollenbrink in the Men's, Schurz touched me on the arm, wiggled a scrap of paper and walked away to an end of the wide hall. I followed him, and there by an open window looking out on the Straits of Florida between two great dangling sheaves of brown palm leaves chattering and hissing and snickering in the wind at our new-born troubles Schurz started in on a licorice-flavored story that I didn't catch the very first of for trying to put my finger on something in our lives the stinking 'Instrument' hadn't annihilated; I hooked on as he went into the loft that morning to feed and water the birds, the rest of the birds.

He moved a disconsolate glance toward what had become the three empty nests of Big Blue, Jake, and Sue Red, hating to do it, he said, as you hate to look at a chair whose usual sitter won't ever sit in it again. Two were still empty but there was Jake in his, so conked out making up sleep he couldn't wake up while Schurz was taking off his capsule, gave Schurz the bleary bottom half of one eye (which Schurz demonstrated). He twisted the wet paper out of the capsule, fingers all thumbs but not tearing it, wiped the premonitory sweat-mist off his bifocals and managed to decipher what I deciphered too when he handed it to me—the words, that is—handed it with, 'My wife tried to iron some of the wrinkles out, Mr. Bennett':

DRY TORTUGAS OFF FT JEFF SEP 28 653 PM
THE CAPTAIN CHATS WITH STRANGERS IN THE CABIN
WHILE BAREFOOT SEAMEN WHISTLING IN THE SHROUDS
ADJUST THE BREEZES TO A METAPHYSICAL T
                              HELGA

I read it again (who wouldn't!) and then again, rubbing the foggy paper between my coarse fingers while I tried to find an adequate word or two of exegesis—perhaps a reference to the infectious nature of the balmy (usually) air of Mr. Schurz's habitat (and Nolan's—and Jake's, indeed); maybe a guarded mention of the now-open-for-business bin we had practically rented; maybe dismissing it all with a simple 'Well, well, Mr. Schurz.' None of which seemed to fill the bill and I finally, handing back the paper, settled for, 'If you think Jake would like to talk to Dr. Mollenbrink I believe it could be arranged—at a figure,' (I didn't feel intimate enough with him to suggest he might well put in a rollaway couch for himself and stretch out too).